WAITING FOR THE CYCLONE

WAITING FOR THE CYCLONE

STORIES

LEESA DEAN

BRINDLE
&GLASS

Edited by Colin Thomas
Cover photography by Francisco Garcia
Cover and interior design by Pete Kohut

LIBRARY AND ARCHIVES CANADA CATALOGUING IN PUBLICATION
Dean, Leesa, author
Waiting for the cyclone : stories / Leesa Dean.

Issued in print and electronic formats.
ISBN 978-1-927366-50-9

I. Title.

PS8607.E24W34 2016   C813'.6   C2016-903303-1

"Waiting for the Cyclone" and "Shelter from the Storm" have
previously been published in the *New Quarterly* magazine.

We acknowledge the financial support of the Government of
Canada through the Canada Book Fund and the Canada Council for
the Arts, and of the Province of British Columbia through the British
Columbia Arts Council and the Book Publishing Tax Credit.

The interior pages of this book have been printed on 100% post-consumer
recycled paper, processed chlorine free, and printed with vegetable-based inks.

PRINTED IN CANADA AT FRIESENS

20 19 18 17 16   1 2 3 4 5

For my family, both chosen and not

CONTENTS

WAITING FOR THE CYCLONE

T HE LAST TIME I SAW Michael was in New York City. It was two years ago, almost to the day. I remember how the Brooklyn Bridge traipsed across the horizon outside the hotel window and the scent of ripe garbage wafted up the fire escape. That morning, Michael and I both ate a grapefruit and half a bagel for breakfast. I remember exactly what I was wearing: jean skirt, yellow shirt, black sandals. Michael wore jeans and Doc Martens and we argued about him wearing boots to the beach.

It was a Sunday, mid-August, too hot. We took the D train to Coney Island and peered at the mismatched architecture when the train emerged above ground—shops with faded awnings, brownstones, postwar ghettos, and grandmotherly houses with dirty windows. I leaned against Michael's shoulder the whole time. He kissed the top of my head and lingered there as if he might forget the smell of my hair once I was gone.

Coney Island was exactly the way I imagined it: slow-driving cars on the boulevard, the smell of sugar-powdered grease in the air. A man with flipper arms played the drums outside the Coney Island Freak Show and a woman in fishnets prowled across a stage, waggling a jar. "Behold the space alien embryo!" she said, thrusting the jar toward us. Inside, there was a glowing fetus with slit eyes.

Michael stopped in front of a ground-floor apartment at a corner on Mermaid Avenue. Behind a paisley curtain, a typewriter sat on a red sixties-style table. The typewriter looked identical to Michael's. A FOR RENT sign was taped inside the window. Michael placed his hand on my stomach the way a man might do to his pregnant wife.

"We could live here this winter," he said.

I knew what he was doing and I didn't like it. I removed his hand from my stomach. Something tugged at the lines on his face, and I thought he might slap me the way he did in bed when I asked him to. I almost wished he would so we could start talking about what was happening to us instead of pretending everything was fine.

We followed the tinny beach music and carnival sounds to the boardwalk. Children were scattered like marbles across the wooden surface. Girls in boxy bikinis waited for their mothers to catch up and little boys stuck out their stomachs and fiddled with their shorts strings. Inside the amusement park, people waited in lines, shifting their weight from one foot to another. Spindly legs hung from rides that spun into the sky and back; screamy open-mouthed laughs rose and fell in unison.

Michael had been on the Cyclone before. On our very first date, in a dark basement bar with old chandeliers, he told me nothing in his life had prepared him for the first drop. When the coaster careened downwards, his jaw clacked with such force that one of his incisors broke. He pulled at the corner of his mouth to show me. I slid close beside him and ran my tongue over the damaged tooth, feeling the bumps like it was my own mouth.

How we met was accidental. I was looking for a ride from Montreal to Halifax on Craigslist and ended up browsing the missed connections. The ad read, *You: riding your bicycle, singing Etta James. Me: at the corner of Duluth and Esplanade, reading* The Heart Is a Lonely Hunter. *We must meet.* I answered on a whim. Michael and I wrote back and forth about the problems of the human spirit and our grandmothers who both came to Canada from Hungary during the revolution. When we finally met, I could tell by the look on his face that he'd seen a different girl riding her bike, but that I was somehow better.

Fast forward through steam-heated nights and whisky-fuelled marriage proposals after three weeks of knowing each other. Linger, perhaps, on a Thursday in

June when we stayed up all night because the first hot day was coming and we wanted to feel the slow, restless vigour of it coming to life. That morning on the roof, bathed in sunlight and sleepy ecstasy, I told Michael he was not allowed to love me. I was moving for school. He laughed and said, "You will never leave me."

Two months later we were in Coney Island spending our last weekend together. It was the kind of day where heat punches you in the stomach. The lineup for the Cyclone stretched all the way past the last souvenir shop. Michael stood beside me with his arms crossed. Perspiration glittered on his forehead and he said it again:

"We could live here this winter."

As the end of summer approached, Michael started to test me. Suggesting plans that would only work if I dropped out of school. "Let's run away to Hungary," he said. "We'll have a gypsy wedding in a dark forest near Vajszlo. Let's build a cabin and live off the land. Anywhere in the world—you choose."

At first, the part of my brain where logic lives started to shake and crack. In the dim glow of his bedside lamp, skin on display, I said, "Let's do it. Fuck everything." But by August, I had an apartment rented in Vancouver.

Michael probably would have come to Vancouver if I'd asked him. Commercial Drive could have been our Mermaid Avenue. We could have sold our meagre everything, skipped town, left our ghosts in Montreal. But I didn't ask. I never wanted to see a tarnished version of what we'd been that summer. The expiry date made us perfect.

WE WAITED FOR the Cyclone for almost an hour. The roller coaster shrieked along the tracks while the riders' screams pinballed through the metal scaffolding. Michael and I didn't talk much. In front of us, a man and woman spoke to each other in sign language. The woman had short grey-blonde hair and her face reminded me of a German soldier I'd seen in a film. Her husband was a thin black man with brassy curls and one pierced ear. I could not imagine what circumstances had brought them together. The woman signed delicately as if she was conducting a small opera; the man's pink palms flashed as his hands laced the air.

"It's a sign," Michael said.

He believed in signs from the universe. Number eights or tigers could mean his life was on track; the number four or wolves could be reason for concern. At first, I was annoyed that someone so intelligent could move through life that way. But I started to see things, too. Once, my bank account balanced to Michael's birthday. Then, just as I was emailing my lease to Vancouver, "Please Don't Go" came on the radio.

For Michael, seeing the deaf couple signified that we were destined to be together. It had something to do with the chapter he was reading in *The Heart Is a Lonely Hunter* when "I" cycled by singing Etta James. I guess he'd forgotten I wasn't actually that girl. I think about her sometimes. It makes me feel weird, like I accidentally stepped into her life. Did she feel a shift when I met Michael? Is she still out there somewhere, silently dealing with the unexplainable weight of a lost opportunity?

Up close, the Cyclone looked fragile with its outdated graphics and weathered paint. Giddy riders climbed out of the sweaty bench seats, still reeling from the speed. The deaf couple sat in front of us. The man was so tall that his knees pressed against the front of the wagon. The woman took a bobby pin from her hair and slipped it into her pocket. Someone swept a video camera over the crowd and zoomed in on each rider. When it was our turn, Michael and I moved our faces together as if posing for a photograph. I could still smell grapefruit on his breath. An employee walked from wagon to wagon and clicked the safety bars into place. Michael moved in close and put his hand between my thighs. I tightened my muscles to keep it there. In front of us, the deaf couple gripped the bar and exchanged a look. It could have been fear, confusion, or something else.

The roller coaster jerked as it climbed and we rose into a crosswind that sent our hair flying. Just past the beach, the Atlantic Ocean stretched and swallowed. There was a pause at the top before the first drop where Michael had broken his tooth. I wanted to kiss him right then so we would both remember how it had been, but it was too late. We were already falling fast.

WHEN THE RIDE was over, Michael slid out of the wagon. I wasn't ready to leave. My stomach had recorded every hairpin turn and rapid descent. I rubbed the muscles along my spine and rolled my shoulders back. The deaf couple was still in the wagon in front of me. Something was wrong. A baffled silence had overtaken the woman's face.

She shook her husband's arm so hard that when she let go, his head struck the front of the wagon. It didn't take long for the strange siren of her distress to fill the air.

"Everybody out," someone ordered. "Clear the area!"

We stayed as close as the park staff would let us. Parents held their children's hands a bit tighter and everyone stretched a few inches taller as if it might change what they saw. The park medics arrived first. The ambulance wasn't far behind. It was clear the man was dead, but none of us could leave until we knew for sure.

AFTER THE AMBULANCE took away the man's body, we didn't feel like going to the beach. Michael unbuttoned his shirt and let it sail as we walked down Surf Avenue toward the D train. I took off my sandals and walked barefoot. When we passed the apartment with the paisley curtains, a man was standing by the window. His chest was caved in like he'd been in a car accident and never fully recovered. You could see his entire life from the sidewalk: one sad plant, a stained futon, and a half-eaten sandwich by the typewriter. When the man looked at me, his tight-lipped stare seemed to say, *You don't want this, missy.*

I still wonder how we looked to him. He might have seen through our relationship the way some people could. Or perhaps he saw the shimmery mirage: how we kissed so many times the night we met, each time swearing it was the last. When we finally let each other go, an audience had gathered around us. People clapped like we were the best thing they'd ever seen, and someone shouted, "Look! They're in love!"

MALAD

TWO WEEKS BEFORE CHRISTMAS, DAD came home from work and said, "Guess what, kids? We're going to Arizona."

"Yeah!" me and Jordan shouted, giving each other high-fives. Next thing we knew, Dad was in the principal's office telling old Bancroft we'd be gone for a while.

The alarms went off at five the next morning. The house sounded like a fire truck! Everyone kept snoozing until Dad got mad and knocked on everyone's doors, yelling, "Get your butts out of bed!"

I jumped up fast and groped for the light switch, but I

couldn't see two inches in front of me. You can really lose yourself in that kind of darkness.

I checked the fridge for juice but the carton was pretty much empty. The house was freezing! I put on Mom's sweater, the one with two dogs balancing on a bowtie, and did some jumping jacks to warm up. Dad paced around the living room while the CD player blasted "Blue Moon." Dad thought it might lure Mom out of bed because she used to love that song. Now all she listens to are annoying tapes with chirping birds and ocean sounds. Dad says it's a mid-life crisis, but I think she's just going nuts. At the dining room table, Jordan shovelled chips into his mouth. "I'm tired," he whined. What a brat. Dad left his USA shopping list on the counter: *Fish smoker, Beef jerky, Bubble lights for the Christmas tree.* You can't get bubble lights in Canada, but Dad knows where to buy them in Missoula. He knows a lot about the USA even though he's Canadian.

Mom and Dad met at a music festival in Nevada. Mom had been living in a tin can trailer with a snake charmer and a fortune teller named Ramona. Ramona had already told Mom about Dad, so love at first sight didn't come as a surprise to anyone but him. I can't imagine Mom living with snakes, but Dad swears it's true. "You should've seen," he said. "All different shapes and sizes. One of the pythons ate the neighbour's dog."

After breakfast, I helped Dad pack up the Subaru. Suitcases, more suitcases, pillows so me and Jordan could have fights, a radar detector, and pork rinds to snack on. Mom was still in bed, even though we were ready to leave.

"Mary!" Dad yelled. "Get your ass out here right now!"

He sent me and Jordan to wait in the car. When he came out with Mom, she was wearing sunglasses, even though it was dark outside. She slid into the passenger seat and put on her seatbelt.

"Everyone buckled up?" she asked.

"Yes!" we said in unison.

Mom twisted around in her seat to check. Jordan had a pillow over his lap.

"Show me," she said.

"It hurts my stomach!" Jordan whined.

"Jordan!" Mom barked. She flipped up her sunglasses and gave him the evil eye. The whites around the irises were cracked like junkyard windshields. She stared him down until he buckled up.

Dad backed the Subaru out of the driveway and accidentally knocked over the neighbour's trash can. He didn't even bother to get out and pick up the garbage.

The car smelled like old Chinese takeout and turpentine—the stench was coming from Mom. Dad sniffed the air and rolled down the window, even though it was snowing. "Hey," Mom said. "You want us to get sick?"

Dad pretended he didn't hear. He just kept his hands on the wheel and whistled like it was a fine, sunny day. You would've thought he was off strolling in a cornfield by himself instead of sitting in the car with the three of us.

THAT NIGHT, WE stopped in a town called Malad. *Malade* in French means "sick." It's one of the few things I remember from French class. I almost said, "Hey, Jordie, it's a town for people like you!" The doctors couldn't decide, but Jordan either had ADD or Tourette's. It must be Tourette's because he's such a spaz. You should see what he does to Mom sometimes. He follows her around the house and wrenches his arm back and forth like he's a trombone player in a marching band. It makes her so mad!

For some reason, Dad chose a pet-friendly hotel even though we left the cat with Grandma. The room smelled like wet fur. Jordan went in first and took an entire bed for himself. He took his Game Boy out of the stupid Big Bird tote he carries around like a baby and barked out every Tetris move, fast and snappy like a sports announcer: "L block comin' in quick, gotta slide in for the home run under the Z block . . . square falling fast, missed it! Strike one, losing ground, code red . . ."

"Told you we should have flown," Mom said.

Dad shrugged and turned on the TV. Mom took a bottle from her suitcase, poured something into a cup, and drank it in one gulp. Then she unrolled her yoga mat. A few months ago, she turned into one of those crazy yoga people. Sometimes we'll be looking all over the house and find her in the basement, tucked into lotus position when she's supposed to be making dinner or helping Jordan with his homework. Even in the kitchen, she alternates between basting the chicken and doing forward bends.

Mom sat cross-legged on her mat, breathing loud

through her nose. Dragon's breath, she called it. Snort snort. Dad perched on the edge of the bed, super excited about all the TV channels. He flipped around for a while until he found something great: *Cops*. Everything was going okay for a while—I read a book, Jordan stayed in his nerd world, and Dad watched TV while Mom snorted on her mat. But then Mom got into a standing pose at a crucial moment during a high-speed chase.

"Hey," Dad said. "Get out of the way."

Mom ignored him. She reached an arm in the air and stretched her fingers wide.

"Mary, for Chrissake, will you move?"

Mom twisted around, turned off the TV, and resumed her pose.

"Jesus fucking Christ!" Dad yelled. I thought he was going to hit Mom, but he just yanked his coat off the bed and shoved on his boots. The door slammed and the windows shook. Mom covered her face with her bony hands. I looked over at Jordan. He was still glued to the Game Boy. Mom didn't move for a while and I wondered if I should say something. Eventually, she grabbed the bottle from her suitcase and went to the bathroom. I heard her lock the door.

I put on my coat and went looking for Dad. Frozen, empty cars filled the parking lot. I thought maybe Dad would be in the Subaru listening to the Beatles or Jimi, but he wasn't.

I went to look in the park behind the hotel. Right in the middle was a small lake with figure eights scratched into the ice, but no one skated. I could see a van parked on the other side with someone in the driver's seat and it made me think about those TV shows where creepy pervs lure kids into their vehicles. The door opened and someone came out. I thought maybe I should run, but then I saw a lady, not a creep.

"Howdy," she said. "Nice night, wouldn't you say?"

"Hi," I said, feeling shy.

"In the summertime there's loons all over that lake. Y'ever heard a loon call?"

"No," I said. "I mean, I'm not sure."

"They sound like this: *ahooo . . . ahooo*. Sometimes I stay up all night listening to them out there, talking to each other. It's really something."

Her name was Maureen. I bet she was old like Mom, but it's hard to tell with some people. She had a nice smoky voice, like a country singer.

"Are you gonna sleep in that van tonight?" I asked.

"Yeah. It's home, y'know? I travel all over the place, working through the warmer seasons. I'm a shroomer."

"Shroomer?"

"Yeah, a shroomer. I pick mushrooms for a living. Morel season starts up in March, then I pick chanterelles in the fall. I dry 'em up and sell 'em to restaurants. I don't work for nobody but myself."

"Do you live in your van?"

She laughed in a way that made me believe she laughed all the time. "I guess I do," she said. "That must seem strange to you, but it makes sense to me. You know where I'm going next?"

"Where?"

"Mexico. On the Pacific Coast, you can camp where you want. I stay down there every winter. Don't that sound nice?"

"That's so cool!" I said.

"It's real easy to live on the beach. You could do it if you wanted. Maybe in a few years. How old are you now?"

"Twelve."

"Really?" she said, eyebrows up. "That's it? I reckoned you was at least a teenager, walking around here by yourself."

"I almost am," I said.

"You got a point there. Either way, if you wanna live on a beach when you get older, you go ahead and live on a beach. People says the world's an oyster and that's damn true. You can do what you want, girl."

As we walked, Maureen told me stories about living in Mexico. She said you can go in the morning and get a fish straight off a boat for a couple dollars. I told her a thing or two about Canada and made up some stuff, too, like when I said we have a woodstove and maple syrup trees in the yard. I wanted her to think my life was interesting.

"It sure ain't warm out here," Maureen said. "I'm thinking tea might be nice. You want some?"

"Sure," I said.

We half-skated across the pond, sliding our feet until we reached the other side. Maureen opened the van's side door—she hadn't bothered to lock it. Bags of dried mushrooms hung from the roof and they made me think of the elf kingdoms in Jordie's video games. Maureen placed the kettle on the stove and turned on the burner. Soon, the air smelled like propane and camomile. Once the water boiled, Maureen pushed up her sleeves and poured hot water into each cup. She didn't use tea bags. Tiny shrivelled flowers bobbed on the water as I sipped. They felt gross in my mouth, but I didn't say anything.

"This is how life should be," Maureen said. "Don't you think?"

"Yep," I agreed, though I really had no idea how life was supposed to be. Mom had gone crazy and Dad yelled all the time. I didn't know if life would ever be good again.

"What are you doing here, anyways?" she asked me. "Shouldn't you be with your folks?"

"Mom and Dad had a fight."

"Oh, I see. That's why I never bothered getting married," Maureen said.

"You don't want a family?"

"Nope. I never did want no husband or kids. Now, I hope you don't take that in a bad way. I just don't have a mothering kind of lifestyle. I'm always on the move."

Maureen didn't say much after that. I tried to think of new stuff to tell her about Canada but ended up thinking about Mom and how she looked tired all the time and drank too much. Sometimes she cried when she made us breakfast. I didn't understand what was happening to her.

Maureen yawned and stretched out on the bed. I knew what was coming. She checked her watch and said, "You'd better get going, little lady, before your folks get worried.

I don't wanna be causing trouble with y'all."

I wondered if Mom had come out of the bathroom yet. Maureen lay on the bed another minute with her eyes closed and I tried to memorize her face because we'd never see each other again. Too soon, she rolled over and put on her coat and boots. The cold burned my cheeks when I got out of the van.

"Take care of yourself, okay?" Maureen said. "You seem like a good kid."

Her puffy jacket made a hissing sound like a tire losing air when we hugged.

My feet crunched on the snow as I walked, almost ran, across the park to stay warm. Back at the hotel, Mom was passed out in an armchair. Dad lounged on the bed eating pork rinds while he watched *David Letterman*. He smiled when I came in but didn't ask where I'd been.

I put on my pyjamas in the bathroom and noticed an empty vodka bottle in the garbage. Jordan and I had to share a bed but I stayed as far away as I could so his bum wouldn't touch me in the night.

The next morning, Mom was still asleep in the chair. The sun came through the window and landed on her face. She looked really nice like that. I bet that's just how she looked when Dad fell in love with her.

WE ARRIVED AT Uncle Jim's house in Arizona the next night. He's Mom's brother. I sort of remember him from when we were kids, but I wasn't even in kindergarten the last time he came to visit. We knew he had a wife named

Debbie but no one had met her. As soon as we pulled into the driveway, we saw her sitting on the front step. I could tell right away she was going to be great.

She stood up as soon as we parked and came to meet us by the car. "What beautiful children!" she said. When she hugged me, I smelled something nice, like the perfume samples you get inside magazines. We all went inside together. Their house was better than ours because it was bigger and they had more than one TV. The best part of all, though, was the swimming pool. I couldn't believe they had their own pool! That night, the adults sat on the patio while me and Jordan swam. Halfway through December and there we were, floating on air mattresses.

Our cousin Cindy was at a friend's house and didn't come home until late. She was Debbie's daughter, not Jim's, so I guess she wasn't really our cousin. She showed up wearing fake leather pants and had a rat perched on her shoulder. The rat's name was Sid, like the singer from the Sex Pistols. Cindy put on her bathing suit and came into the pool. She was only a year older but she had breasts, unlike me. Cindy strutted down the diving board, bounced once, and sailed into the water. I watched her torpedo past in a comet of blue bubbles. I wanted to dive like that, but my legs kept smacking the water every time I tried. We swam until our skin wrinkled and then we went to bed. That night, I felt better than I had in a long time.

THE NEXT MORNING, Dad came into the room. I couldn't tell what time it was because of the dark curtains, but it felt really early. Dad was wearing his Scooby-Doo shirt—I could tell even in the dark. It's my favourite.

"You sleep okay, kiddo?"

"I'm still sleeping," I grumbled.

"You don't have to get up," he said. "I just want to tell you something. Your mother and I are going away for a few days."

"What?" I asked.

"Your mother and I. We need to leave. It'll only be for a few days."

"Why?"

"We just need a bit of time alone. Be good for Jim and Debbie, okay?" Dad gave me a pat on the shoulder.

"Is Mom sick?" I felt stupid asking but I needed to know.

"She's just having a hard time, honey." Dad leaned over and gave me a smooch on the forehead.

"Love you, kiddo," he said.

I had a terrible feeling he might come back without Mom. I felt like crying but waited until he left.

THE FIRST DAY without parents was strange. Jordan seemed okay but I kept thinking about when Dad first told me and Jordan about the trip. I thought it was going to be a family vacation. Debbie felt bad for us, I could tell. She asked lots of questions about school and our friends back home and let us do things like eat ice cream out the carton and go to bed without brushing our teeth. Cindy still had school during the day but she said I could play with Sid whenever I wanted. Sometimes in the afternoon,

I brought him to the yard and made him obstacle courses out of toilet paper rolls. Other times, I did stuff with Debbie, like shop for groceries and get my toenails painted by professionals.

On Saturday night, a tour guide named Oscar drove me, Debbie, Jordan, and Cindy out to the desert in a Hummer. It was so cool! The dashboard had all kinds of screens like a spaceship, and it sounded like a fighter plane when we drove fast. Oscar drove through the city until there were no lights, and then he turned onto a road where sand swished under the tires. The trees had crazy arms and sharp needles that stuck out all over the place. "They're called mesquite trees," Oscar said. Sometimes they have to dig their roots a hundred feet for water. They have to work hard, but they're determined to survive.

Cindy and Jordan ran off to look for coyotes, but I stayed behind with Debbie. We sat on the hood of the Hummer and looked at the night sky, all lit up with stars. There were so many of them all crowded together and it made me think of a star forest. I also thought of a story Mom read to me as a kid, about a lady who stole the night sky and made a sparkly dress out of it. Debbie told me some stuff about constellations. "That one's Andromeda," she said, pointing to a sideways V. "Someone chained her to a rock to be eaten by a sea monster."

"Did she die?" I asked.

"No," Debbie said. "Someone saved her."

Nobody wanted to leave the desert, but Oscar said we had to go. He sounded angry. We found out later it was because Jordan broke his compass. Back at the house, Cindy threw down her backpack and said, "Last one in the pool is a douchebag!" We ran for our bathing suits, bumping into each other in the hall. Mine was still wet from my afternoon swim so I inched the soggy bottoms over my hips and ran into the pool. When I came up after my dive, Cindy was staring at me. She had a look on her face that turned into a nasty smirk.

"Baby tits!" she squealed, pointing to my chest.

I looked down and saw that my bikini top had come undone.

I jumped out of the pool and ran to the bathroom as fast as I could. The door was jammed so I threw myself against it. When the door swung open, I saw Debbie on the toilet seat. She had a syringe dangling from her hand, and one of Jim's neckties flopped over her knee.

"What's the trouble, doll?" she asked. Her eyes looked fake and shiny, like the clear rocks at the bottom of aquariums.

"Something stupid happened," I told her.

Debbie laughed. Her voice twinkled like a Christmas star. She didn't even notice I was missing half my bathing suit. I pointed to my chest. She stared in wonder.

"Where's the other half?"

"It fell off in the pool."

Debbie slid from the toilet to the floor. She held a hand out to me. I took it and sat beside her.

"Cindy called me baby tits," I said.

"Oh honey," she crooned. "Don't listen to her. Breasts

are no big deal." Debbie looked down at her own chest. "These aren't real, you know." She started to undo the pearl buttons on her blouse.

"They were supposed to be nice," she said.

She opened her blouse. There was a gaping scar under her left breast. It was dark purple, almost black, the way bruises are when you first get them. It looked like it hurt. I reached out and ran my fingers along the scar. Debbie leaned back against the wall. I snatched my hand away, embarrassed. She sat there with her blouse hanging open, staring at the space between the toilet and sink.

"Why do you take needles?" I asked.

"I have a medical condition."

"Do you have diabetes?" A boy I knew at school had to give himself needles every day because of it.

"Something like that," she said with her eyes half-closed. I could tell she wanted to be alone. I took a towel from the linen closet and wrapped it around my bare chest. Then I went to my room so I could be alone, too. Debbie knocked on the door a while later and asked if I wanted to watch a movie. Her eyes were back to normal and she acted like nothing had happened. We made popcorn and watched *Wayne's World* with Cindy and Jordan, and even Uncle Jim hung out with us. I couldn't stop laughing at the movie, and Uncle Jim told me I laugh just like Mom. We all went to bed late. It took me a while to get to sleep. I kept thinking about what happened with Debbie.

I decided not to tell anyone what happened.

MOM AND DAD came back a week later. Just like the first night, the parents spent the evening beside the pool with drinks while us kids swam. I knew it was going to be really hard to say goodbye. Cindy and I became friends after the pool incident and did some cool stuff like go to a roller rink where men in coloured spandex did figure skating routines. We went back to the desert, too, but not with a tour guide. It was just me, Jordan, Jim, and Debbie.

I didn't want to get up on departure day, but Dad did his usual door knocking and yelling thing. We all ate cereal and toast and drank juice by the pool. No one said much except Debbie. She tried to cheer us up by reading jokes from the morning paper. In the driveway, she hugged me so tight I could feel her bones.

"Come back any time, doll," she said. "You're always welcome here."

I looked out the back window as we drove away until Debbie got too small to see. Dad put on the radio and Mom didn't nag him about flipping between stations. They'd stopped fighting since they came back and I wondered if things would be different once we got home. Maybe we'd be a real family again. Me and Jordan were exhausted from staying up late every night and we both fell asleep in the car. When I woke up later, Mom and Dad were talking. I kept my eyes closed so they wouldn't know I was listening.

"Jim told me Debbie lost her nursing licence," Mom said. "They caught her stealing from the pharmacy."

"Hmm," Dad said.

"We shouldn't have left Janet and Jordan with her. She's a junkie."

"The kids were fine," Dad said.

Mom snorted. "Jim told me Cindy stepped on one of her needles. He's just about had it with her."

I didn't believe anything Mom said. Junkies were dirty people who hung around the clock tower downtown and ate in soup kitchens. Once, a man came to our school and told us he used to be a junkie. He showed his scars and said he got AIDS from dirty needles. People like Debbie were not junkies. I knew that for sure. I wanted to defend her, but I was supposed to be sleeping.

It started to rain. We stopped at a drive-thru once everyone got hungry and ate our burgers in the car. Dad wanted to make it to Malad before midnight, so he drove really fast. I rested my head against the window and closed my eyes. I thought about home and wondered what it would feel like to be there again. The house would be cold and there would be snow.

I was almost asleep when I heard Mom's voice over the windshield wipers.

". . . we'll just tell them I'm going away, okay? I don't want to make a big drama out of it."

"Mary. This is dramatic. There will be serious consequences," Dad said.

"It hasn't been easy for me. You know that."

"Seems pretty easy now, doesn't it?"

"Paul, Please."

"You need help. Running away won't fix anything."

"That's not what I'm doing."

"Think of the kids for once."

"You think they like me this way?"

"Nobody likes you this way."

Jordan sat up and started moving around, so Mom and Dad stopped talking. He took out his Game Boy and started to play one of his wizard games. He kept the volume down low, but I could still hear the stupid music. I wanted to throw him and the Game Boy out the window. As long as Jordan was awake, I knew Mom and Dad wouldn't talk again. I really wanted to know when Mom was leaving and how soon she'd be back and if she was going away to get better.

We arrived in Malad after midnight. Dad pulled off the highway and parked in front of the hotel office. He came out with two separate keys: one for the girls and one for the boys. Me and Mom took our suitcases and watched Dad and Jordan go into a room together. Mom left her stuff by the door and lay down on the bed in her clothes. I sat on the other bed. I didn't want to get too close in case she wanted space, but I wanted to be near in case she needed me.

I could hear her crying even though she tried to hide it. I took a chance and sat beside her. There's this thing she sometimes did when I was a kid where she scrunched her hand and walked her fingers down my arm like a spider. It was her way of saying, *Hey. You're okay.* I thought maybe it would help. While I did the spider thing, I told her all the best stuff that happened since we left home, like meeting

Maureen who picked mushrooms and lived on the beach. "I want to live on a beach someday," I told Mom. "Maybe we could do it together." I told her about the desert at night with all the stars and how it reminded me of the story she used to read me before bed.

"Do you remember?" I asked.

"Yes," she said. "Of course I do."

She took my hand and brought me close to her. Each of her fingers felt like a hard bone—she'd lost so much weight it scared me. I lay beside her for the whole night. Eventually Mom fell asleep, but it took me a long time to wind down. There were too many thoughts in my head. So much had gone on since we left, and so much more was going to happen. I thought about all the possibilities; in the end, I decided I would accept whatever it would take for Mom to be happy again. Through the walls I heard Jordan and Dad watching TV, and I knew that from then on I would be in a house of men.

TIEBREAKER

CHRISTIAN WAS NOT PLANNING TO pick up any hitchhikers until he saw a woman at the roadside wearing a big hat like some kind of movie star. She looked like the type a travelling man would pick up and leave beaten in a cornfield. He pulled over because he didn't want to feel guilty about it later.

"Thanks," the woman said, leaning through the passenger window. Her black hair was so long it touched the seat.

"Put that in the trunk if you want," Christian said, motioning to her suitcase.

"No," she said. "I like to keep my things close."

The suitcase was small and yellow. There couldn't have been much in it. She placed it flat on the floor and put her feet on top. Her shoes were red.

"Where you headed?" he asked.

"Creston. You?"

"Osoyoos. I can drop you off on the way."

"That would be lovely, if you don't mind."

"Ain't no trouble."

Christian lit a cigarette once they were back on the road. The woman reached into her purse and pulled out her own pack. They sat in silence while the wind rifled through the window and made their cigarettes crackle.

"Where'd you come from today?" she asked, taking a drag.

"Calgary. Was up in Fort Mac yesterday, though."

"Working?"

"Yeah. I'm done now."

"How is it up there?"

Good question, he thought. Loud. Depressing. He'd planned to quit after the first contract. That it was happening now, a decade later, was just bad luck. His grandmother was sick. He'd probably be back wrenching pipes once she was either well or dead.

"I don't know," he said. "Nothing special."

"You don't look like someone who'd work up there."

"What's that supposed to mean?"

"Hey, don't get mad. I just mean you don't look like one of *those* guys. It's a compliment."

What the hell did she know about it? Probably nothing.

She looked like the kind of girl who never got her hands dirty.

"Thanks," he said. "I guess."

"Osoyoos," she said to change the subject. "Is that where you live?"

"When I'm not in Fort Mac."

"I was there on Canada Day last year," she said. "There was a big party on the beach. Most of the people were from Quebec, ironically. Someone told me they were fruit pickers who worked at the orchards outside of town, but all I know is they were crazy. They stayed up all night playing violins and accordions and shot Roman candles at each other. It was a really wild time!"

"I don't get out much," Christian said.

The woman laughed even though he was being serious. Her lips parted to show a row of small, sharp teeth. Christian tried to remember the last time he'd driven around with a woman. It had been a while. He looked at her, sitting half prim and proper, half like a slouched teenager. She could be eighteen or thirty. It was hard to tell with some people. It didn't matter much anyway. She'd be out of the car by Creston and forget she ever met him.

HE'S A WEIRD one, Valery thought. On the surface, he looked like a clean-cut nobody with a boring life. Groomed hair, department store clothes, rosary hanging from the rear-view mirror. But there were tattoos on his knuckles. Black squares, probably covering something. Ex-lover's name? A bad word? There was something unsettling about his face, too, that suggested a guilty conscience.

He looked like one of those people whose life was stuck between two currents.

She stared at the tattoos, stretched by his grip on the wheel. Christian noticed. Valery looked away. Outside the window, the highway curved with the Bow River and she thought of all the road trips she and her brother, Ben, had taken to Calgary. They'd both continued living with their parents after high school. Neither went to college. Those were the years of colossal money-wasting and all-day hangovers. Eventually, their parents kicked them out.

During the drive, Ben liked to narrate the landscape. He told of mine explosions and grisly murders in small towns. "Imagine the sound," Ben said to Valery in Frank, a town that had been wiped out when a mountain fell in the night. "Like a storm through a megaphone. It'd come at you too quick to even think. Blood, Val. Shooting from your eye sockets like Old Faithful." Ben was like that— always trying to coax others into being as morose as he was. The image had stayed with her. Sometimes at night she would lie in bed, heart racing, expecting a mountain to come and pulverize her.

But now he was getting married. No one had expected a marriage in the family, especially not from Ben. Many times he'd declared he'd rather die than spend his life trying to please a woman. Valery hadn't met the fiancée but others had. She tried to imagine what kind of woman might decide to share a life with her brother. All she could think of was variations of Sylvia Plath, but apparently the girl was normal. That's what everyone said. Happy even. People told her Ben was happy, too.

Valery looked at Christian again. He wasn't a talker. She couldn't figure out why he'd picked her up.

"Tell me something about yourself," Valery said.

"Not much to know."

"Oh, come on."

"I don't know what to tell you."

His face remained composed but Valery noticed a change in his tone. Not annoyance but something else.

"Fine," she said. "I'll tell you something first. But then it's your turn."

He didn't respond.

Valery thought about what to say. Humour worked with most people, but with him it might fall flat. She decided to risk it.

"I once took a crap in the ocean," she told him.

"That's weird."

She looked at him. Was he smiling?

"It was in Mexico. I was camping with friends," she explained. "We were broke, and it cost money to use the toilet. Every day was an ordeal, looking for a place to, you know. One day I was swimming and the surf was high and I thought, *This might work.*"

He was definitely smiling.

"I swam until I couldn't touch anymore and . . . did the deed. Afterwards, I swam back to the shore. At first, things were fine. Totally status quo. I relaxed and took out a magazine. It wasn't long, though, before I heard a shriek.

I looked up. Someone was pointing at the water. There was my turd, bobbing toward the shore."

"Shit," the man said.

They both laughed.

"It was awful! Every time I thought it had sunk or drifted, it showed up again. I had to leave the beach."

Once she finished her story, Valery lounged back in the seat. Christian fiddled with the dial, looking for a radio station amongst the static. Valery folded down the sun visor and applied a fresh coat of lipstick, pursing her lips at her reflection. Christian watched her with an amused expression that made him look handsome. What if they were at a bar? Would she hit on him? Possibly. He took his hand off the wheel and for a second she thought he might place it on her knee.

He was only reaching for his cigarettes.

THE SMELL OF gasoline seared through Christian's nostrils as he pushed the nozzle into the tank. They were in Radium. *How quickly things change*, he thought. *She tells me a funny story about shitting in the ocean and I end up talking about my fucked-up life.*

"I used to be a bad person," he told her.

"What do you mean? Have you, like, killed people?"

He said no, but that wasn't exactly the truth.

"What's the worst thing you ever did?" she asked.

"I can't tell you that."

"Fine. How about something medium bad?"

"I crushed a guy's hand for a mickey of rye."

She sucked in her breath. "Ouch."

Her reaction was disapproving, but she also started flirting. Tossing her hair like she was in some kind of shampoo commercial. She kicked off her shoes and took off her movie star hat. He couldn't decide if she looked better with or without it—she looked good either way.

"Were you a thief?" she asked him.

"Big time."

"What's the biggest thing you ever stole?"

"Twenty thousand dollars."

"What? How?"

"From a safe."

"Seriously? You know how to crack codes?"

"It's not hard."

"You never got caught?"

"No."

"Wow," she said. "You're like James Bond."

He didn't like where the conversation was going. Things were different now. He was a better man than he used to be.

"I never got caught," he said, "but things have happened to me over the years. Bad things."

"Like what?"

"I've been shit-kicked within an inch of my life."

She looked at him with wide eyes.

"Got stabbed once, too. Probably had that coming. I've got a list in there of all the stuff I've done and all the stuff that's happened." Christian rapped his knuckles against the glovebox. "I'm almost even," he told her.

I'VE BEEN SHIT-KICKED within an inch of my life. Valery immediately thought of her brother and something that happened in high school. It had been years since she'd thought of the incident, but there it was, clear as the day it happened. Ben was going to a house party near St. Mary's School. Valery was invited, too. Ben had to work late so they arranged to meet there. After his shift, he cut through Kinsmen Park. As he crossed the soccer field, someone whistled from the creek banks.

"Down here, dude! Come have a toke!"

Ben thought it was someone he knew from school. He walked over, swinging his bag of beer. Three guys were waiting for him. One took away Ben's alcohol and pushed him to the ground. Another kicked him in the face while someone rifled through his wallet. They kicked him in the ribs and back. "I thought I might die," Ben later told Valery. Eventually they stopped kicking and rolled his body into the creek. Ben lay in the frigid water until they went away.

At the party, people jumped from the roof into the pool and hotboxed the bedrooms. Valery danced with the older boys and gave one a blow job in the downstairs bathroom. She kept looking for Ben but he didn't come. That night, she slept at a friend's. Her mother called in the morning to tell her what happened.

Valery was hungover and Ben was high on painkillers. She crept into his room and sat beside the bed, dizzy from the shock. Ben's left arm was in a sling, folded like a chicken wing. His face had been stitched where tread from the attacker's boots had torn open his skin. Two teeth were missing.

"I'll find them," Valery promised. "I'll find them and kill them."

Something else was going on, too. It was sick the way Valery felt aroused when Christian told her about the beatings. Why did she have the urge to slip one of his hands, those former instruments of torture, under her dress? She looked out the window so Christian wouldn't see.

"You said you're from Osoyoos?" she asked.

"No. That's where my grandmother lives."

"Where'd you grow up?"

"Kamloops, mostly. Sometimes Williams Lake."

Good, she thought. When they'd started talking, she'd wondered. But he couldn't have attacked Ben. No way was he that guy.

CHRISTIAN LIT ANOTHER cigarette. Ever since the woman started asking questions, he felt the need to chain-smoke. She made him nervous. There was something disconcerting about her. The way she talked to him like they actually knew each other. That and her eyes were always roving around, landing on things. Receipts on the dashboard, cassettes, even old coffee cups. Plus she kept looking at his tattoos.

Every day, he remembered how they'd looked, done with a Bic and a safety pin in a friend's basement. Hurt like hell. When he got them covered years later, the guy pressed the ink gun hard. Made the squares extra black, extra deep.

Hurt even worse than the first time. The guy didn't say a word until he was done. Then he took Christian's money and pointed to the door. "Get the fuck out," he said. "Nazi piece of shit."

"HEY, DO YOU mind if we stop for a few minutes?" Valery asked. They'd just passed a sign for a rest area.

"No problem." Christian flicked the turn signal. Valery put her shoes back on and adjusted her hat in the mirror, tilting it slightly to one side. They were past Fairmont, driving through a dead zone between tourist towns. Narrow strips of farmland bordered one side of the road. The Columbia Basin was on the other. Most of the land was for sale. When they were kids, Valery and Ben had fantasized about having their own ranch.

"We could have a thousand horses!"

"And live like Billy the Kid!"

"Grow a million Christmas trees!"

"And decorate all of them!"

They'd usually stopped at the same rest area on their way to Calgary. Once, Ben found a snake. He picked it up by the tail. Valery had watched in horror as it pretzelled around Ben's fingers and snapped its tiny jaws.

The parking lot was deserted. Christian turned off the engine and removed the keys from the ignition. He unbuckled his seat belt and put the keys in his pocket.

"Hey," Valery said.

"Yeah?"

"Thanks."

"For what?"

"I don't know. For the ride. For telling me all that stuff."

"Just keep it to yourself," Christian said.

They sat in silence, not quite looking at each other but not looking away. Valery got out of the car when she realized he wasn't going to try anything. She climbed a bristly, desert-like hill and stood at the top, taking in the panoramic view. Columbia Lake was the colour of laundry detergent. Across the water, a rusting cattle trailer sat empty on the hillside. Horses pawed at dry patches in the grass and flicked their tails. Christian stood close beside her.

"I always wanted to live around here instead of Cranbrook," Valery murmured.

"You're not from Creston?" Christian asked.

"No. That's just where my brother's getting married. We grew up Cranbrook."

"Funny. I lived there for a while."

"In Cranbrook?"

"Yeah."

"When?"

"Years ago. Haven't been back since, except for gas."

"Why didn't you tell me? I asked where you lived!"

"I wasn't there long. Not even a year."

"When were you there?" she demanded.

"I don't know. Maybe fifteen years ago?"

"What year?"

"I don't remember."

"Was it 1999?"

"I don't remember. It was a long time ago."

"Think. I'm sure you can figure it out."

"Why is this important?"

"I need to know. Please." Valery watched his face as he scanned through his memory, patching together a spotty chronology of a life left behind.

"Yeah," he finally said. "It was 1999."

CHRISTIAN COULDN'T FIGURE Valery out. In the parking lot, she was giving signals. Strong ones. He could've kissed her, no problem. Now she was acting like he'd done something terrible. After he told her he'd lived in Cranbrook, she turned and ran. When he caught up, she was circling around the car, trying to get in. The doors were locked. Christian unlocked her side first. She looked anxious. Angry even. The first thing she did when she got in the car was open the glove compartment.

"Don't," he said.

She closed it.

They got back on the road. Valery kept her mouth shut. They'd been getting along so well. Had they met before? Maybe he'd done something to her. He wondered how to start the conversation again. He could ask what she was doing for dinner. He needed to get to Osoyoos, but a few hours wouldn't make a difference. They could stop somewhere nice.

She'd probably say no.

"Let me look," Valery said, pointing to the glove compartment.

"No."

Before he could stop her, she had it open again.

"Hey," he said. She pushed his hand away.

"'June 1998, Kamloops,'" she read from his list. "'Stole two hundred dollars from Grandma, spent it on drugs.' Oh, that's nice."

"Stop," he said. "I'm serious."

If he'd done something to her—there was nowhere to pull over. The road was too windy, too unpredictable. He took the corners fast, hoping for a straight stretch.

"'December 1998, near Blood Nation. Beat a hitchhiker with a shovel. Might've died, not sure.'" Her voice lowered when she said *died*.

"Stop it," he said.

"'June 1999,'" she continued. "'Cranbrook. Beat some-one up and threw him in the river.' That was my brother, you asshole."

He veered toward the curb and hit the brakes. Valery was out before the car reached a full stop. Her shoes crunched on the gravel as she ran. Christian turned off the engine and stood by the car. "Hey!" he called out. Valery ignored him. What were the chances? He cupped his hands to shield the wind as he lit a cigarette. It could have been someone else. He knew other people who got up to no good in Kinsmen at night.

"It might not have been me!" he yelled.

But it could have been. Either way, at least he hadn't done something to her. Christian leaned through the open window and picked up the list, left crumpled on the seat. For years, he'd carried it in his shirt pocket, made notes, watched the columns equal out. He was almost even. *December 2002, near Golden,* he read. *Car caught on fire with me in it. July 2007, Edmonton. Stabbed in the chest by a crackhead.*

"Let me talk to you for a second!"

To his surprise, Valery turned around. He watched as she walked back toward the car. A long, black strand of hair divided her face and her cat eyes glared. She was beautiful.

"It could have been someone else," Christian said. Her face registered no emotion. He took her hand. She didn't resist. He lifted his shirt. There was a small but deep scar on his stomach above the navel. He placed her hand on the scar tissue.

"I've been through shit you can't even imagine," he said.

Valery raised her chin. There they were again. Her probing, searching eyes. What was she looking for? She put pressure on the scar and for a moment he thought she might kiss him. He closed his eyes and waited for it.

She pushed him.

"Go to hell," she said.

She took her suitcase and left. Christian sat in the car for a long time afterwards, holding the list in his hand. In the rear-view mirror, he watched Valery put out her thumb. It didn't take long for someone to pick her up. He watched as the car accelerated and disappeared around the next corner. Christian smoothed his list on the dashboard. He recounted both columns. Twenty-one, twenty-one. Exactly even. There was a pen in his shirt pocket. He took it out and began to write: *August 2016, near Fairmont.*

LIBERTAD

THE LAST THING ALISON REMEMBERED was the fire show. A woman with blonde dreadlocks whipped gaslit chains in fast pirouettes, leaving traces of flame around her body. She filled her mouth with kerosene, arched her back, and sent a whoosh of flame hurling past the crowd. Such a bright, burning sound! People gasped, their open mouths glowing as the flame passed. But what happened next, Alison didn't know. All she could remember was the smoky grey sky once the fires went out.

In retrospect, going to the bar had been a mistake. Trance-like music and red lights had beckoned David and

Alison from their nightly walk along the beach. Inside, people danced like marionettes with red-stained teeth. "Viva Mexico!" someone shouted. A woman wove through the crowd with a tray of tequila shots, shimmery barrettes taming her curly hair. She beelined for David and Alison, handing them each a shot and a slice of lime. The woman looked at David and spread her thumb and forefinger wide. "Lick," she told him, salting it. He hesitated, giving Alison a sidelong glance.

"Go on," Alison said.

The woman closed her eyes as David ran his tongue across her skin. Alison slapped him on the bum. "Bad boy," she said.

Bad boy and bad girl. "Careful," David had warned when Alison took a second shot. She had a tendency to drink too fast, too much, until her memory became a maze to untangle the next morning. She couldn't quite remember getting back to the hotel. What time had they gone to bed? David would know. She stretched a hand under the covers and reached for his arm.

It wasn't David's arm.

She opened her eyes. Beside her lay a stranger. She couldn't see his face, but he had shoulder-length black hair. The Mayan tattoo on his left arm was so vivid it felt like she was looking through the door of a temple. Across his shoulder blades, tattooed in gothic letters, was the word *Libertad*.

She scanned the room, looking for clues. Tunnels of light punched through the driftwood walls, leaving striated patterns on the floor. There were no windows. A salt-stained surfboard leaned against the wall and a pair of shorts draped over the fin. Alison's dress lay on the floor. She pulled back the covers and slipped out of bed, careful not to disturb the man. Her panties were missing but she didn't care. She needed to get the hell out of there. Still, she paused in the doorway before leaving so she could look at the man's face.

He was handsome.

THE DRIFTWOOD BUILDING was actually a hotel. It looked like it had been built by pirates. Dream catchers and mobiles dangled from cage-like balconies, and tiny seashells spelled out *Posada la Palma* over the entrance. On the roof, there was a sculpture of a man and woman walking on a plank. The woman wore a dress of torn bedsheets and the man's suit jacket was a sun-bleached version of white. Between the two figures, a man with an eye patch stood holding a tangled blonde wig. *I'm dreaming*, Alison thought. *This can't be real.* The man placed the wig on the woman's skeletal head and draped the curls over her shoulders.

He looked down at Alison and held her gaze.

She turned and ran along the beach, past a fisherman who sat at the hull of his boat, repairing a damaged net. Alison avoided eye contact when she passed, her flimsy sandals twisting with each footfall. What had she done? She thought of the tattooed man, his hard jawline and muscular body. She ran until she reached a cliff. A narrow trail made switchbacks through prickly underbrush to the top. When she arrived there, she looked down. Plastic cups and beer bottles glittered in the sand—she recognized where the party had been the night before.

David was on the beach. Although he had his back to Alison, she could tell by his motions that he was trying to describe her to people. Some avoided him, startled by his sweeping gestures. Alison hid behind a boulder and watched him make his way down the beach, continuing to question people, unsteady as he walked. A colt, she thought, still finding his footing.

Once he was far enough away, Alison followed the trail down the cliff and went to where the party had been. A bucket of water propped open the back door. She entered the bar and was hit by the strong smell of bleach and half-smoked cigarettes. A woman mopped the floor while she listened to the radio, but there was no music, just a man speaking in Spanish. She sloshed the mop under a plastic chair where it collected cigarette butts in its dank fibres. Alison then remembered something—she'd sat in that chair the night before while David spoke to some woman from Alabama. Alison had been forced to converse with the boring husband, a finance lawyer and proud Republican. She'd ordered drinks whenever the waitress came by, hoping it would make the conversation more bearable. It didn't.

It seemed to go on for a long time, David and that woman talking. Her laughter seemed fake, eager to please. Alison had drifted in and out of the conversation, offering curt responses to the husband's banal questions. She'd looked past him to the woman with the blonde dreadlocks on the dance floor—the way she moved was both provocative and private. She looked the same later, on the beach, spinning her firelit chains.

"*Estamos cerrados*," the woman with the mop said to Alison, motioning for her to leave. Alison looked around the bar one last time, hoping for clues, but she didn't remember much else. Outside, she circled the building and stopped in front of a cluster of palm trees.

That man. He'd kissed her there.

She recalled his hand up her skirt, his unshaved chin rough on her neck. But why? Why had they been alone together?

She remembered telling him no.

"*Sí*," he'd murmured, then kissed her again.

DUST ROSE IN dry gusts under Alison's feet as she walked along the unpaved road connecting the beach to the village. She passed a row of shabby cantinas with handwritten menus, still closed that early in the morning. All she wanted to do was lie down. She coughed and spat into the dirt as if the action would somehow vindicate her. When she arrived at the hotel, David wasn't there. Alison looked at herself in the mirror. Hair in tangles, smeared mascara. Filthy. She licked a finger and rubbed under her eyes until the smudges dissolved. There was a cold half-cup of coffee on the counter. Alison took it and drank it, walking toward the unmade bed to sit down. A dark bruise had formed above her knee. She pulled up the hem of her dress and put pressure on the mark. It only hurt a little. She took off her dress and sat naked, investigating her body. Another bruise appeared further up her leg, and Alison noticed a red, circular mark on her thigh.

Teeth.

Alison searched for long pyjamas to hide the marks but of course all she had were shorts. They were in Mexico. Her head hurt and she felt nauseated. She lay down on the bed and thought about what to tell David. Everything she came up with sounded like a lie, but the truth was not an option.

WHEN ALISON WOKE up, the clock beside the bed flashed red numbers that were supposed to mean something. There was an arm around her. It was David's arm.

"Where were you?" he asked.

Alison closed her eyes. She didn't answer the question. How could she? *I passed out*, she imagined saying. *The bartender put me in a room.*

"Are you hurt?" David asked.

I went into the wrong hotel room and fell asleep. I was so tired I didn't notice.

"Did someone do something to you?"

No, she wanted to say. The words wouldn't come.

"Do we need to call the police? Come on, Ali, talk to me."

"No," she finally said.

David began to pace the room. He was wearing the same clothes as the night before. "Where were you?" he asked.

None of it made sense. If she'd kissed another man, if she'd been able to leave with him, it meant David was not there. Had he gone somewhere with the woman from Alabama? No. He wouldn't have.

"I shouldn't have left you," David said.

"I don't understand. Where did you go?"

"You don't remember?"

"No. Nothing."

David remained silent, thinking about his response before speaking. Alison studied his face. The crow's feet were deep and there was a smattering of grey at his temples. He was getting old. They both were.

"I ran out of cigarettes," he said. "You were talking with Kathy and George, so I came to get another pack—"

"Kathy and George?"

"You know, the couple from Alabama."

"You left me with those two?"

"Hey, you said you wanted to stay."

"I'm sorry," Alison said, "I'm trying to figure this out. So, you went to get cigarettes and left me with Kathy and George."

"Just tell me where you were, Alison."

"How long did you leave me?"

"It was a mistake," he said.

The bed had been unmade when she returned. His scent was all over the sheets. She imagined him the night before, taking off his shoes and lying down, not thinking about her at all.

"You came back here and went to sleep, didn't you?"

David looked away. "I was drunk. Not as bad as you but . . . I didn't mean to fall asleep."

They were both quiet. David fidgeted with his watch and Alison looked out the window. In the backyard, birds with long, oily tail feathers hopped through the garden. A hotel chambermaid hung damp sheets on a clothesline. In the distance, Alison heard a pickup truck idling by the town square. "*Pochutla!*" The driver yelled. "*Pochutla!*"

"Just tell me where you were," David pleaded. "I was so worried."

"Nowhere," Alison responded. "I fell asleep somewhere, woke up, and came right back."

It wasn't exactly the truth, but it wasn't a lie, either.

ALISON CLOSED HER eyes and tried to ignore David's presence. He said her name once, but she lay still, pretending to be asleep. Eventually, he took his cigarettes and left. As she lay there, images from her life collapsed into a tight stream—there was David at twenty-three, a newscaster at the radio station where she'd volunteered in high school. He was five years older and had big dreams of running his own station one day. Alison had been young, unsure of herself, but certain about David. They'd fallen in love too quickly.

Over the years, despite their best intentions, they'd become less interesting people. David kept reporting on the weather, on minor traffic jams, playing whatever hits people requested. Alison moved from job to job, first as a secretary and then as an executive assistant. They talked about moving once or twice. "We could go somewhere with better opportunities," David said. Once, he came home with a job posting for a station in Austin. "The music scene there," he told Alison. "It's out of this world!"

Alison wanted to leave, but when she tried to imagine herself being American—Texan specifically—she couldn't stop laughing. In the end, David didn't apply for the job.

As she got older, Alison wondered what it might be like to be with someone else. She'd only ever been with David. Occasionally, she flirted with other men. David was a flirt, too. "You should dance with her," she'd said a few times at parties, pointing to women she knew he found attractive. They teased each other, knowing neither would act on their desires.

Until now. What had she done with that man? She couldn't remember anything past the kiss.

It wasn't fair. She wanted to remember everything.

DAVID WAS BACK at the hotel before long. Alison heard the Velcro of his sandals, his bare feet on the tiles. Soon, she sensed him beside the bed. To move would be to initiate conversation and she wasn't ready to talk. The blankets had shifted, leaving one of her legs exposed. Only then did she remember the bite mark. She felt his fingers brush against it, circling the contour of the raised skin.

David slammed the door on his way out. Through the screen, Alison watched him take fast drags of a cigarette. The noxious odour drifted into the room and made her stomach turn. She knew him so well, but not well enough to know what to say. She pushed back the covers and slowly brought herself to a sitting position. She felt weak and out of sorts, but nonetheless stood to walk to the bathroom. There, she took off her clothes and stepped into the shower. Water trickled in a weak stream and she soaked a washcloth so she could scrub her body. Clean water ran into the cloth and dirty water spiralled down the drain. She moved a hand between her legs, washing once, then again. Had they at least used a condom?

She stayed in the shower for a long time and considered what she could tell David. Eventually, she turned off the water and stepped onto the shower mat. There was a mirror on the wall. She looked at herself, really looked for the first time in a long time, and wondered why the man had chosen her the night before. Did he think she was pretty? She turned to the side and touched her breasts. They were sore. Had the man squeezed them? Put them in his mouth?

"What happened last night?"

She turned around to find David standing in the doorway, shoulders tensed. Alison grabbed a towel and tightened it around her body. She walked past him and looked for something to wear, something that would look nice, but all her clothes seemed boring. Some of her dresses were garish, with sailboats and tropical flowers. When had she become that kind of person?

"I asked you a question," David said.

She looked at him, standing there with his arms crossed.

"Don't you dare," she said, rooting through her suitcase. "You're the one who screwed up."

"Tell me what you did last night!"

"You left me," Alison said, turning to face him. "That's what happened. I bet you didn't even come back here. You probably brought that woman from Alabama somewhere and fucked her."

David raised his hand and slapped her. Not hard, but just enough to make a point. She touched her face where his hand had struck. She could feel the heat of the mark. Emotions divided David's body into hemispheres; his face showed remorse but his body still looked primed with anger.

"Ali. God. I'm sorry."

She hadn't meant what she said, but still, there was something satisfying about lashing out. She'd always been a good wife, never raised her voice. Yelling felt good, even if she was being unreasonable. At first, when she saw him standing in the doorway, she'd considered telling the truth. She could tell David she was sorry.

No, she thought. *Let's try something different.* She went back into the bathroom and locked the door. She sat with her back against the cold tiles and pulled sections of her hair—an old habit. "Don't," David said whenever he caught her. "It's self-destructive." Outside, the pickup truck idled through town again. Alison heard the driver call "*Pochutla! Pochutla!*" The next morning, she and David would be in that truck, heading to the airport, heading home.

The trip had been David's idea. "We'll take a week off," he'd said. "Get away from it all." Alison agreed only because she'd been in shock, and in that state, agreeing was easier than disagreeing. For years, they'd tried for a child. She'd never expected it would take so long to get pregnant. She definitely didn't expect it to end the way it did.

"Lots of women miscarry in the first three months," David had told her, thinking it was a good thing to say. It was not.

He knocked at the bathroom door. "Ali, I'm sorry. Okay? Open the door."

It was their last day in Mazunte. At home, she knew they'd settle back into their old routines. Eventually, David would want to try for another child. But Alison didn't want to try again. The process, the possibilities—it was all too painful.

"You must be starving," David said, voice losing energy. "We should get some dinner."

The idea of walking through the village made her nervous and excited. Would she run into the man? Would he say something? Probably not. But he might look at her a certain way. Alison knew that David would push the incident from his thoughts until it no longer existed. She, on the other hand, would be applying mascara or walking the dog years later and she'd catch herself thinking about that man in the driftwood hotel, trying to recall something, anything at all.

THEY WENT FOR dinner in a restaurant near their hotel. Alison ate everything on her plate. She was starting to feel stronger, less nauseated. "We're leaving tomorrow," David told the owner, a man named Alejandro who'd been very kind to them.

"*Qué triste*," Alejandro said, shaking hands with both of them. After dinner, they walked from the village to the beach, passing houses where families grilled meat over charcoal pits. Stray dogs lingered nearby, skin tight over their washboard ribs. Along the shore, tiny shells and creatures left stranded by the tide were strewn across the wet sand. Luminous haze from distant ships cast white shadows over the wrinkled sea. Ahead, Alison saw the bar where they'd been, but the front door was closed and locked.

"Let's walk a bit further," Alison said, pointing to the cliff.

David followed Alison to the end of the beach where the trail started. The tide was high. Water churned through slick black rocks before it was taken back to sea. As soon as they reached the top of the cliff, the driftwood hotel became visible. David stopped walking and stared, perplexed by its strangeness. Alison continued on the trail and David followed until they reached the hotel's entrance, lit by a dim lantern. At night, the dream catchers looked like spiderwebs. David ran his hand along one of the gnarled driftwood beams, while Alison tapped a finger against a seashell mobile and listened to the haunting echo.

"*Buenas noches*," a voice said from behind.

Alison spun around. The man with the eye patch was standing there, smoking a cigar. He looked at David and Alison with a bemused expression before casting his gaze to the flotsam sculptures above. Bright spotlights made their white clothes radiate, and the halogen glow illuminated the spaces between their bony fingers. From that angle, the figures looked like they were dancing along the plank instead of walking to their death.

"They're beautiful," Alison said.

The man took a haul of his cigar and exhaled through his teeth. "It is my son who makes this art," he said. Alison felt her cheeks turn pink at the mention of his son.

"Juan Riviera," he continued. "He is famous."

His name—Juan. Now she remembered. He'd repeated it three times in the bedroom, an incantation. She looked away. David noticed the change in Alison. He was reminded of a date early in their relationship, a sudden flush, a coy smile across the table. It wasn't until later that he realized it was for the waiter, not him.

"We have to go," David said to the man. He took Alison's arm and led her away from the strange hotel. Once they were far enough down the beach, he stopped and faced Alison.

"You were here last night," he stated.

Alison nodded.

His face showed disappointment and relief. He let go of her arm and walked ahead by himself. As the distance between them grew, Alison thought of her lover and his bedroom, the light bursting through the walls as she gathered her clothes in the morning.

David waited by the cliff for Alison. He would always wait for her, that she knew. Before she joined him, she looked back at the hotel one last time. Maybe her panties were still trapped in the sheets.

THE FOUR BRADLEYS

LIZZY

Tonight is Rock 'n' Roll night at the Legion so I get to
hang out with Dad and the band. They call themselves
the Four Bradleys, but I think that's silly because our
last name is Bradley and the bass player's first name is
Bradley, but the other two are Jimmy and Dave. I asked
Dad what's up with that and he said, "That's a very good
question, Lizzy. It's something we do in the music indus-
try. Basically," he said, "we're just like the Ramones." I
have no idea what he's even talking about!

Candace is supposed to help me get ready for the big

night but instead she's moping in her room wearing really short shorts. They make Dad crazy! He's told her a million times, "Candace, you are not allowed to wear those shorts," and "Candace, your mother would not approve." Today he said, "Candace, you are insufferable," because she wouldn't eat dinner. Dad made KD and hot dogs—and salad too—but Candace said she's doing a fast to raise money for charity. When Dad asked which one, she said, "I don't know, all of them." Then I heard her eating chips in her room.

I'm going to wear one of Mom's dresses tonight, the blue one with the droopy sleeves and a pink flower on the front. Candace says it makes me look like an orphan but I don't care. It still smells like Mom and it makes me look like a princess. At least that's what Vern says. He's Dad's friend and he sits with me while Dad's onstage. Sometimes Barb comes, too. That's Charlene's Mom. Charlene is my BFF. Barb's only got one leg but she's still pretty cool and she can dance just as good as someone with two legs. When me and Vern dance, Mom's dress wobbles as I spin and spin and it makes me feel like an island surrounded by waves!

I'm a real good dancer, like Mom. She used to be a ballerina. I asked her over and over if I could pretty please wear the shoes just once and she said no way José but I kept asking until she finally said yes. Boy, was that a joke. I couldn't even stand up! Mom laughed so hard she sounded like a choking horse, but she promised I could take real dance classes once she was back from Afghanistan. I can't wait!

Tonight's Rock 'n' Roll night at the Legion but I'm not going. It used to be fun, but now it's just depressing. Me and Mom used to sit together and make jokes about Dad's band, the Four Bradleys. They're just a bar band, but the way Dad struts around the stage, you'd think they were the Rolling Stones or something. Mom and I used to play this game where we'd clap extra loud for all the worst songs. Once, she took some plastic flowers out of a vase and threw them at the stage. "Bravo!" she shouted. "Encore!" God, that was funny. People thought she was being serious.

Everyone is still shocked about what happened. Last week, Brad the bass player had a breakdown. Most of the time I don't mind Brad. He's kind of a cool guy and he's usually pretty funny, but not last week. We were playing pool together. After I sunk the eight ball, I called him a sucker and gave him a punch in the arm just like Mom used to do. I thought he'd laugh, but he started to cry in a bad way. Poor Brad.

When she said she was going to Afghanistan, I was so confused. It's not like she's in the army or anything. Her plan was to volunteer at a pottery studio for women who'd lost their husbands in the war. On March 15th, my birthday, she should have come home. If she'd have flown back on time, she'd still be alive. Instead, she decided to stay an extra month. On the 19th, she went to the mountains to dig clay, and while she was out there, a rock came loose and hit her in the head. At least that's what Dad said. But I keep wondering, how big was the rock? Didn't she hear it?

Was it really a rock or did something bad happen and no one's telling the truth? I'm thinking terrorists. Gunshots. Blood on the ground.

No one wants to talk about what happened. Sometimes Lizzy says she misses Mom, but that's about it. No one's asking questions as far as I can tell, or maybe everyone's asking questions. How would I know? I've tried talking to Dad, but whenever I bring up the subject, he raises a hand and says, "Don't."

She called home the day before she died. There was a lot of noise in the background and the line kept breaking up. It sounded like she was calling from a million miles away. "I won't be home for your birthday," she shouted. We'd planned a trip to the city—shopping, a hotel, tickets for my favourite band. Even if we rescheduled, I'd miss the concert. I was so mad. "I hate you," I told her.

The phone cut out right after, or maybe she hung up.

RON

I've been thinking a lot about something Brad said after he found out his wife had cancer and couldn't have kids. We were eating double bacons and fries at Burger Island when his fork snapped in half. He looked at it and said, "This is my life, Ron. A broken fork." That was a couple years back. Brad kept talking about his disappointing life, and even though I felt sorry for the guy, I couldn't help but feel smug. My life, I thought, was not a broken fork.

Yeah, right.

In March, I got a phone call from a woman in Turkey who

told me my wife was dead. "Dead?" I responded. "Turkey? You must have the wrong guy." The woman on the phone said, "Listen, sir, we have her passport. Donna Rae Bradley, born in '62? I'm sorry. She's been in a parasailing accident."

Parasailing? She was supposed to be volunteering for some pottery thing in Afghanistan. God. All that crap about how *committed* she was to her students, how she just *couldn't bear* to leave until they finished the course. Was Donna ever in Afghanistan? You know, she went to Mexico for some kind of house-building project before the kids were born.

I wonder if that was a little vacation, too. Okay, fine. There were pictures from Afghanistan on her camera. But there were also pictures of her at the beach, draped all over some beefy jerk.

Things were bad before she left. We weren't getting along and I kept asking, "What's the matter?" She'd say, "Nothing," in that special voice women use. There's nothing a man can do when a woman gets like that. You just have to hope whatever storm your wife's in will blow over. We'd talked about counselling and then all of a sudden Donna was going to Afghanistan. Said it'd give her time to think about things. I remember saying, "Things? What things?" But she wasn't ready to talk. Married fifteen years and she didn't want to talk. Go figure.

Donna'd been away before, but never that long. The day she left, I dropped Lizzy off at Charlene's and stayed to chat with Barb. I thought she'd have some advice on single parenting. I've known Barb just as long as Donna.

We've all been running around together since high school, but last year Barb got in a bad accident. She lost a leg and her husband. I don't envy her one bit, trapped in the car with her dead husband until help came, not to mention the leg. That kind of thing can really throw you for a loop.

Me and Donna looked after Charlene while Barb was in the hospital. Sometimes if Donna was working, I'd go visit. Barb's a real drinker. It just about killed her, being away from the bottle that long. I'd bring a flask and after a few slugs she'd joke about getting an eye patch and a parrot to go with the leg. Cracked me up every time. I can tell you for certain there'd never been anything between me and Barb. I never thought she was pretty, but she changed after the accident. Everyone agrees: tragedy looks good on her.

So Donna was off in Afghanistan doing arts and crafts and I was alone, trying to manage the kids. Bringing Lizzy to Charlene's kept me from going crazy. I'd stay for drinks with Barb while the kids watched TV in the other room. It was all fine until one Sunday we had a few too many mimosas and Barb was trying to read my palm. The way she touched me after all those months alone? It didn't take much to cross the line.

Soon enough, Barb started coming to Rock 'n' Roll night. It was real nice, having her there. In a way, we felt like family. Things hadn't been good with Donna for ages. You know, after the year we both had, Barb and I needed that time together. I haven't seen her since the funeral, though. She won't call and she won't come around. When I bring Lizzy over to play, Charlene tells me her mom's busy.

I don't know what I'm supposed to do.

Lately, I've been trying to focus on the band to keep my mind off things. We had a lot of fun over the years—me, Donna, the band, everyone we know. When we first started going around together, Donna used to dance up front with the band girlfriends. She was the best of all of them. One night, I pushed her home in a grocery cart while she sang "Hang On Sloopy." God, was she a beauty.

I want to remember her that way.

The band's been doing "Oh Donna" every week down at the Legion. That was Brad's idea, but I can't anymore. I'm upset and overwhelmed with the kids and I don't know what's going on with Barb. I wish she'd at least call. Last week onstage I caught myself looking at the door, hoping she'd come around. It's enough to drive a man crazy.

LIZZY

It's just past eight and Dad's already onstage, making doo-wop sounds with the microphone. Check one-two! Candace wouldn't come so it's just me and Vern. He just told me the funniest joke: What do you call a pig who knows karate? A pork chop!

Dad's a totally different guy up there onstage. People laugh at his jokes and he wears fancy clothes. Tonight, he's wearing a leather coat he bought off the Indians. The band plays lots of Beach Boys stuff and they always play "Sea Cruise." Dad really gets into it. He does the *oooh-eee, oooh-eee baby!* just like the real singer. He takes the microphone off the stand and walks around going *oooh-eee* to all the ladies. They just love my dad. They turn red and toss their hair every time he comes by. Sometimes Dad holds out the microphone and gets them to sing along. You should hear some of those old buzzards try and croak a tune!

The last song of the night is always "Oh Donna," the one from the *La Bamba* movie. Dad does this thing where he gets them to turn down the lights; then he clears his throat, and says in a very special voice, "As many of you know, I recently lost my wife in Afghanistan. This song is for her." When Dad starts to sing, the room gets real quiet. Nobody says anything until he's done.

Dad always looks at the pool tables by the back door while he sings and I know he's looking for Mom. Sometimes I look, too. Mom liked to play pool. I keep hoping I'll see her there, lining up for the shot. It could happen, you know.

CANDACE

Dad and Lizzy finally left. They tried to guilt me into going tonight, but I told them I feel dizzy from all the fasting. "I don't like the sounds of that," Dad said. "I'm fine," I insisted. "It's for the children in Africa. Mom would be proud, don't you think?" He left me alone as soon as I mentioned her.

I like having the house to myself. Without Lizzy and Dad around, I can feel Mom's presence. The stove is still crusted with sauce from the last time she made pasta and one of her grocery lists is on the fridge—milk, eggs, Cheerios, juice. She usually forgot the juice. Her spare purse is beside the magazine rack, but there's not much in it. Just some keys that don't fit any of our locks. We've been trying to figure out what they're for, but nobody knows.

I had a dream about her last night. She was sitting on a wooden dock, wearing her favourite blue dress. The sun was low in the sky and a fishing boat rocked on the waves. "Come," she said, patting beside her. I buried my face in her sleeve like I did when I was young and told her I was sorry for what I'd said on the phone. She just smiled and said, "I was a teenager too, you know."

In the dream, she told me she was in a place called Pochutla. I remember that name. It's where she went to build houses before she had us kids. She used to talk about it a lot. And guess what? Right beside Pochutla, there's a town called Port Angel. No wonder she seemed happy in the dream. She's probably in heaven.

BRADLEY

A letter came in the mail not long after Ron told me what happened. There was a picture in there of a mosque, bright turquoise, effervescent in the sunlight. Donna sat on the front steps with her legs folded to one side—the most beautiful woman I'd ever seen. In the letter, she said she was going to leave Ron. I think she was serious this time.

I never loved a woman the way I loved Donna. Not even my wife. I keep thinking about the two of us in my apartment, the one above the country bar on George Street, how we'd make love while she was supposed to be at school. She was my favourite.

The worst mistake I ever made was losing her. I drank too much, flirted with other women. Eventually, she went off with Ron. I could barely hold myself together at their wedding. God, was she something in that dress. It should have been me up there. Eventually I found myself a nice girl in town and we got married, too. What else could a man do? Ron was in the wedding party, and Donna sat in the front row. It took everything I had not to look at her when I said *I do.*

Ten years later, we all went camping at Mineral Lake. Donna was pregnant with Lizzy and Candace was in second grade. Early in the day, Ron picked a fight with Donna. I saw her behind the outhouse afterwards and asked if she was okay. "No," she said. I held her in my arms while she cried. That night, she asked me to collect firewood with her. Everyone else stayed at the camp, including my wife. Dave played "I Am the Walrus" on his beat-up six-string while Ron yelled *Coocoocachoo coocoocachoo!* We stumbled through the trees until we couldn't see the fire no more and then Donna pushed me up against a tree. "Kiss me, kiss me like you used to," she said. She had her fingers in my hair and tugged at my belt and I remember thinking, *God, this is it.*

Then she changed her mind.

Jimmy got married later that year. Donna was one of the bridesmaids, all dressed in blue, even more beautiful than at her own wedding. I followed her into the bathroom that night and said, "Finish what you started, young lady."

It's been months and I still can't imagine my life without her. I want to be there for Ron—I do—but I don't feel right about everything that's happened. I'm thinking I should quit the band, maybe leave town. Go down south or something. And those kids. Lizzy's been wearing Donna's clothes to the Legion, and Candace . . . well, she looks like an exact—and I mean *exact*—replica of Donna at sixteen. I just want to take her in my arms.

The last evening I spent with Donna was at the old racetrack. It was just the two of us by the sagging bleachers and faded billboards. We put a blanket in the middle where the grass had gone wild and pretended we were on a beach in Mexico. Afterwards, I lay with my hand on her belly and wished to God we could've had children together.

PROVERBS

AMY PACES THE LENGTH OF the airport's pickup area, on the lookout for a woman named Sharon. She checks her watch—9:27 PM. Either Sharon's late or Amy's given her the wrong flight information, which is possible given her scattered tendencies of late. There's one other person outside—a man with a tight grip on his suitcase, wearing the anxious look of someone who's been forgotten. When he lights a cigarette, Amy considers asking for one. It might take the edge off. But once she gets a look at his face, she won't go near him.

It can't be the man she's thinking of, but the similarities

are enough to keep her away. She drops her backpack on the furthest bench where a local teenager has scratched RURAL TORTURE into the paint. Amy keeps her head down and pretends to read, willing herself not to look at the man's clean-shaven face, his salt-and-pepper hair. Before long, a rusted Hyundai pulls up beside her. The driver is not a woman named Sharon. It's a man in a Hawaiian shirt who tells her to get in the car.

"Who are you?" Amy asks.

"Your new boss."

"Where's Sharon?"

"She's gone." He takes her backpack and puts it in the trunk.

"What do you mean?"

"I mean she's gone. Left yesterday morning. Sometimes she does this. She might be back, might not. You still get your job, though, no worries there."

There are rolling papers on the dashboard and the car smells like weed. They coast out of the parking lot, passing the man who still waits with his suitcase. Along the road to Kelowna, wide canopied trees dot the land-scape, still fruitless so early in the season. Night air hisses through a crack in the windshield as they drive. Paul talks over it, giving Amy the rundown on places to see and things to do in the city. He lists what they grow on the farm and explains what kind of work Amy will do for the summer.

"I'm not sure if Sharon told you," Paul says, "but you'll be sharing a cabin with this girl named Michelle.

She's been here about a month now. Don't worry, she's fine. Ain't nothing wrong with her. She just talks a lot."

"Oh," Amy says, caught off guard yet again. What she wanted for the summer was a place to think and be alone. She wanted to be far from Toronto, and the job posting had asked for someone willing to work and live in an isolated environment. In their email exchanges, Sharon had seemed like the kind of person who would leave her alone. Had she known she'd be working for some guy in a Hawaiian shirt and living with some girl, she might not have taken the job.

Paul flicks the turn signal and pulls into a rutted driveway. A wide veranda laced by dark foliage spans the front of the house. "Home sweet home," Paul says, except Amy's home will be a small cabin pushed against the far edge of the property. Eight by ten, no electricity. Perfect if there wasn't some girl named Michelle already living in it.

Paul hands Amy a flashlight and explains how to get to the cabin. Amy follows a dirt trail past a chicken coop and a few sheds. Acres of newly planted crops, still damp from the sprinklers, create a checkerboard pattern all the way to the fence. From across the field, the cabin looks like a child's playhouse. It's too tall and skinny, like something you might buy in a catalogue.

Amy opens the door quietly, pointing the flashlight at the ground. "Up here," an eager voice says. Michelle's long hair tumbles from the loft and brushes against the ladder. Amy's backpack shifts awkwardly as she climbs, holding the rails tight. Michelle offers Amy her hand, but she doesn't take it. It would only throw her off balance. She arrives at the top of the stairs and realizes she can't stand up straight. The roof is too low.

"I'm glad you're here," Michelle says. "After dinner I caught myself talking to the eggplants. What am I, nuts?"

She talks nonstop while Amy attempts to get organized, though it's nearly impossible without proper lighting. By the time she's arranged her clothes in a pile, she knows where Michelle's from, that she's studying anthropology at UBC, and that she lived in Africa for eight months.

"So what's your story?" Michelle asks.

"I'm from Toronto."

"And?"

"I don't know. That's it, I guess." Amy fakes a yawn.

"Oh geez," Michelle says. "You're exhausted and here I am, talking your ear off. What time is it in Toronto? Like, midnight?"

"Closer to one."

Amy takes off her pants and adds them to the pile. She'll sleep in her T-shirt, the one she wore when she hugged her boyfriend goodbye at the airport.

"I've been getting up at six to do yoga with Paul," Michelle says. "Do you want me to wake you up tomorrow?"

"I'm not much of a morning person," Amy responds.

"Oh. I'll try and be quiet, then."

Amy lies on her stomach and tries to get comfortable. Instead of Matt's scent, the pillow emits a musty cabin smell. It feels strange to be in bed without him, even if their relationship has been strained since the spring. He didn't want her to go away, but she didn't give him a choice.

"There's one more thing you should know about me," Michelle says. *God*, Amy thinks. *Here we go.* Michelle's words come slow, then fast. "I often have to pee in the night. I keep a bucket in here because the barn's so far up the hill. Of course, if that would bother you, I could go outside. Really, that's probably what I should do."

"It's fine," Amy says. "I'm sure I'll sleep through it."

"You probably think I'm weird. People have said that my whole life."

"No," Amy lies. "I don't think you're weird."

Michelle is quiet after that but Amy doesn't fall asleep immediately. The night sounds are so different from what she's used to—at home, there is traffic and raccoons on the neighbour's garage, their tiny claws scratching the shingles. There is also Matt, a night owl surfing the internet, clicking the mouse and rolling his chair on the hardwood floor. Here, the windup clock ticks and she wonders if she'll ever get used to it. Somewhere in the distance is the clink of a chain and a low howl. The neighbourhood dogs all join in, one at a time, yipping like miserable wolves under a sliver moon.

A BRASSY CLANG reverberates through the cabin early the next morning. Amy covers her ears but Michelle snoozes through the racket. When Amy can no longer stand it, she reaches over Michelle and turns off the alarm.

"Sorry," Michelle says, woken by the silence.

"Next time," Amy says, "I'll throw it out the window."

In Toronto, three hours ahead, she'd be stepping off the streetcar at Queen and Dufferin for work if she hadn't quit her job. Amy rolls over and closes her eyes. She hears Michelle leave and falls back asleep, promising herself she'll wake up in fifteen minutes. By the time she actually gets out of bed, Michelle's already done her yoga, eaten breakfast, and started weeding the onion patch. A men's work shirt hangs loose from her body and there's a batik scarf twisted around her head. When she leans forward, the shirt lifts to expose a string of glass beads around her waist. They catch the sun and flash.

"Howdy, pardner," Michelle says.

Amy gives her a two-fingered wave before heading to the main barn, which is also Paul's pottery workshop with a full kitchen and bathroom. After a long shower, she stands in the kitchen, wondering what she's supposed to eat. There's a bag of organic bread on the counter. She takes a slice and looks for a toaster, but can't find one so she sets the oven's burner to high. She threads a fork through the bread and hovers the slice above the glowing element, feeling the heat on her hand.

Can I do this? She wonders as she eats the dry toast on the veranda, overlooking the weed-strangled field. Paul, wearing a hippie skirt of some kind, is standing beside Michelle. Amy knows his type. In Toronto, his habitat would be Kensington Market or any park with a drum circle. He stands there for quite a while, long enough for Amy to finish her toast and drink a glass of water. Michelle sits at his feet the whole time like a faithful devotee.

Amy is in the kitchen washing dishes when Paul comes, wanting to show her around the farm.

"Sharon used to do all this," he tells her as they walk to a greenhouse up the hill. Amy hadn't noticed it the night before. A pout forms on Paul's lips, and for a moment, she actually feels sorry for him. "She's left before," he says, "but this time she took the dog."

He unhooks the padlock and motions for Amy to enter. She is almost entirely expecting a grow-op, but instead she is faced with multiple layers of what looks like grass.

"Catnip?" Amy guesses. It's the first thing that came to mind.

Paul laughs for a long time. She notices the lines around his eyes and thinks he might be older than she thought. Maybe fifty?

"It's wheatgrass," he tells her. He takes a tray that's ready to be harvested and flips it to show her the intricate maze of roots. "It only took eight days to become this complex." He puts the tray back on the shelf and adjusts the spray gun. He pulls the trigger and walks slowly along the rows, misting the wheatgrass.

"Sharon told me you're in a choir?" he asks.

Amy scans her memory, trying to remember when she would have mentioned it. "I used to be. Why?"

"She used to sing in here every morning, but I can't carry a tune. The wheatgrass grows faster if it's exposed to music."

Amy feels laughter brewing and suppresses it. "You're serious?"

"Very. Sharon started last year and the plants have been ready to harvest a day earlier on average."

Amy shrugs. "I can try. Do I have to sing anything particular? Do the plants have a preferred genre?"

"I have no idea. Just sing whatever you want; if the plants don't grow, try something else."

He gives her a pat on the back before leaving, which she finds patronizing. Even though she has no audience but the wheatgrass, she feels self-conscious. She opens the greenhouse door to make sure Paul is nowhere near and sees him on the veranda, drinking coffee. *Does he do anything besides hang out?* she wonders.

Instead of singing, she lies on the ground and closes her eyes. She's still jet-lagged, exhausted from all the changes in her life. She falls asleep for the rest of the morning, lulled by the earthy smell of roots and fresh grass. No one comes to check on her.

THAT NIGHT, MICHELLE cooks dinner for Amy. She's like a mad witch doctor, simmering canned tomatoes and eggplants in a cauldron with too many spices. She cooks in bare feet, and when she walks back and forth to the sink Amy can see her filthy heels. Michelle spoons the concoction into bowls, likely made by Paul, and they eat on the stoop, facing the fields. The meal's not terrible, but it's not great, either.

"Paul told me you're the new plant singer," Michelle says, spooning food into her mouth. A clump of rice lands on her shirt. She brushes it away, leaving a turmeric stain.

"I suppose I am," Amy responds.

"Well? Aren't you excited? It's quite an honour!"

"I think it's dumb," Amy admits.

Michelle shoots her a look. "Don't let Paul hear you say that," she says, her voice low.

Amy raises her hands in the air in mock surrender and wonders if Michelle would jump off a cliff if Paul asked her to. *Probably.*

"I'm entitled to my own opinion, aren't I?"

"Sure," Michelle says, "but you just got here. Maybe it's a bit early to judge?"

She's right, Amy thinks. Instead, she says, "No, I'm pretty sure if you ask me in a month, I'll still think the wheatgrass singing is dumb."

Instead of laughing, Michelle silently collects the dishes and washes them. It's late by the time they've put everything away, so they retire to the cabin. The mountains are pink edged and the sky is reminiscent of its former blue. Amy's hands feel stiff from all the afternoon's weeding. Since there's no electricity, they each light a candle.

"I'm going to write a letter," Michelle announces. She dips a ridiculous, oversized feather pen into a vial of brown ink. As she writes, a strand of hair detours a little too close to the candle. Amy imagines her engulfed in flames, a comet of smoke burning through the night. The chamber pot is in the same place as the night before— Michelle forgot to empty it in the morning. *If she catches on fire*, Amy thinks, *I'll douse her with it.*

"Got a fella back home?" Michelle asks.

"Um, yeah," Amy says.

"You don't sound so sure."

"It just took me a bit to remember what 'fella' means. Pretty sure no one's used that word in fifty years."

Michelle ignores the sarcasm and says, "My boyfriend—husband, actually—lives in Ghana."

Amy raises her eyebrows. "You're *married?*"

"Sure am."

"Where's your ring?"

"That's not the custom." Michelle rolls onto her back and lifts her shirt to expose the string of beads around her waist. "They're from Mensah's sisters. To welcome me to the family."

"Isn't that nice. Ever considered he might be using you?"

"I assure you, he's not."

"I'm just saying I've heard stories."

"Well, whatever you've heard does not apply to me and Mensah."

"You might want to watch yourself," Amy says. "Just in case."

Michelle returns to her world of ink and paper, slightly ruffled. As Amy listens to the cadence of pen strokes, she considers writing to Matt. It could be a ritual, the two of them writing letters to their faraway men by candlelight. But how would she start the letter? Dear Matt? Hey babe? No. Neither seemed right. She promised she'd write, and she did intend to, but not yet. Not until she knew what to say.

IT DOESN'T TAKE long for Amy to fall into a rhythm—wake up at six, snooze for half an hour, consider not getting out of bed at all; collect eggs from the chicken coop on the way to the barn, cook one and eat it with toast, slow-roasted over the burner; boil water for tea but ice it once steeped; sing to the wheatgrass; get a bucket and tools from the shed; find the solar radio and tune into CBC; pick a field to weed—sometimes with Michelle, sometimes far from Michelle, depending on how she's feeling.

They usually break for lunch at noon. Most of the time, Paul joins them and bores them with stories about his past life as a beach bum in Nicaragua and Thailand. He shows them scars on his legs and back from a shark attack he survived. As the weather heats up, he spends more time standing around shirtless, lord of his fields. Amy finds it annoying, but Michelle loves it.

Today, it's just Amy and Michelle because Paul has gone to Penticton to float the river channel. After their morning yoga, Michelle helped him make sandwiches and load up his truck. Amy saw her contributing some of their shared food to his picnic lunch.

"You shouldn't give him food," she scolds. "He can afford his own."

Michelle ignores the comment and eats her salad. Afterwards, she coerces Amy into Ghanaian lessons. For the first month Amy refused, but Michelle finally wore her down.

"*Wezon*," she says, bowing to Amy.

"*Wezon*," Amy responds.

"*Eti sen?*"

"*Ya,*" Amy responds.

"*Eh ya,*" Michelle corrects.

"Whatever. Same thing."

Michelle ignores the comment and says, "I've got one for you. Listen. *Aɖu wu kplim a?* Now repeat."

"Too complex," Amy says. "Keep it simple or I quit."

"Want to know what it means?"

"No, not really."

"It means 'Will you dance with me?'"

"That's random," Amy says.

"Hey, it might come in handy someday! In Ghana, a man offered me forty cows and an acre of land to marry him. That is a very good offer!"

"Wow," Amy says. "Sounds like everyone there wanted a piece of you."

Michelle hesitates before responding. "I was popular there. In Canada, men never really looked at me. This one guy in high school even said I looked like a stork, with my twiggy legs and puffed stomach. Can you imagine?"

Oh my, you are pathetic, Amy catches herself thinking. She tries to shoo away the thought, to be compassionate the way she'd like to be. But her disdain lingers, persistent like the weeds choking the fields and the dirt living under her nails.

WHILE ON THE farm, Amy is supposed to figure out what to do with her life after the summer. She's narrowed the choices to either continuing her studies or going on a long trip, probably to Europe or Mexico. Part of the decision will be influenced by whether or not she decides to stay with Matt. Every time she tries to come up with a plan, though, her thoughts circle back to what happened in the spring.

In February, Matt and his ex-girlfriend hooked up while Amy was out of town. She agonized over it for weeks, plagued by images of the former couple in rapture, imagining the things they might have done to each other. Finally, Amy decided she would have to cheat on Matt if their relationship was to survive. On March 21st, one of Amy's friends was having a party. It was the kind of party Matt wouldn't go to. Amy decided she'd wear a dress Matt liked so that afterwards, she could tell him she wore it when she fucked someone else. *It just happened,* she'd tell him. *We were drunk.* It's exactly what Matt had said about his ex-girlfriend.

At the party, Amy drank fast and talked to all the men, moving on if they had girlfriends or seemed disinterested. The plan was not going well. Some had girlfriends and others were put off by her forwardness. Just when she thought nothing would happen, she sensed a man giving her a vibe. His salt-and-pepper hair made him look older than he was. The man approached Amy and asked why he'd never seen her around.

"I've been around," she said. "Guess you weren't paying attention." She feigned interest as he poured her drinks and talked about the local art scene and a recent trip to Germany. Later, he said he had to leave but invited her back to his place.

His car was silver and he kept it clean. There was no evidence of daily life—no coffee cups or parking stubs, nothing in the back seat. German industrial techno vibrated through the speakers and the man kept talking about his trip and all the galleries in Berlin. Amy felt nauseated from all the drinks and thought she might be sick. At the corner of Bloor and Bathurst, she asked the man to stop so she could use the bathroom.

It was busy inside the Pizza Pizza. A group of teenagers shoved each other as they waited for their order, and some of the tables were occupied by tired-looking homeless people. Amy walked down the hall to the women's washroom. In the mirror, she saw a disappointing version of herself. Suddenly, she felt exhausted and wanted to go home. She debated whether to tell the man she'd changed her mind or just stay in the bathroom until he realized he'd been ditched.

Before she could decide, there was a knock at the door. "Just a minute," Amy said. She washed her hands. There was no paper towel so she wiped her palms on her dress. When she opened the door, the man from the party came in and locked the door behind him.

"No," she said, pushing him away.

"Shut up," he said.

He turned her around so she was facing the mirror. Her wrists were so skinny he could hold them behind her back with just one hand. He reached up her dress and pulled her panties to the side. She kept her eyes down so she wouldn't have to see any of it. The counter was cold and wet against her cheek when he pushed her face into it and she thought, *This is what you get.*

A LETTER FROM Matt arrives at the end of June. *Hey babe*, it says, *things just aren't the same around here. The city is restless, it's hot, everyone at the Ship is like, we miss Amy! I keep saying, yeah, tell me about it!* His efforts to pretend everything is normal are heartbreaking. She reads the letter twice and thinks about where she can go to be alone, with no chance of running into Michelle or Paul. On her way to the greenhouse, she passes Michelle, sitting straight-backed in the onion patch. She waves Amy over. Amy sighs and settles in beside her, bum in the dirt, surprised by how her willingness to get her regular clothes dirty grows over time.

"I miss Mensah," she says. "We still haven't heard from immigration. I don't know how much longer I can wait."

"Matt sent me a letter," Amy tells her. "He asked why I never call. I don't know what to say." Michelle knows the first part of what happened in March, but not the rest.

"In Ghana, they would tell you *atadi bia ha no le eme.* You can find a worm, even in a ripe pepper."

"I don't get it."

"No matter how bad a situation is, one must cope."

"Oh yeah? Those Africans. Always looking on the bright side."

"You know what else they say? *Aɖu wu kplim a!*"

Michelle kicks off her shoes and begins to dance through the onion patch over to the eggplants. *Oh-ey-*

yay-ah! she sings, thrusting her hands in front of her chest like she's doing push-ups. Amy watches her move through the crops and remembers how she and Matt used to play old records and dance in the living room together. *I got you babe*, he'd sing, hand firm as he twirled her. She thinks of how she'd left the taxi the night of the party and saw him through the living room window, still awake. He called her name when he heard the door open. When she didn't answer, he came to the hallway where he found her on the floor. He tried to pry her hands from her face but stopped when she said no. He stayed with her, talking and then not talking, until he convinced her to come to bed. He put one of his T-shirts over her dress and tucked her in. All night, he would not let her go.

MICHELLE LOSES AT rock-paper-scissors, which means she's in charge of dinner. She and Amy walk through the fields, looking for vegetables that are ready to harvest. Only the lettuce is in full bloom. Amy tries to discourage Michelle from putting it in the stir-fry but she won't listen. Dinner is mediocre yet again. Paul shows up just as they're dishing out dinner, which is something that happens often.

"Sharon and I got married ten years ago today," he says, picking out a slimy leaf. He throws it on the floor, forgetting he no longer has a dog to eat the scraps.

"Have you heard from her yet?" Michelle asks.

"Nothing. But my instincts tell me she'll send a postcard soon from New Mexico." .

"You know," Amy interrupts, not in the mood for Paul's stories, "Michelle got married last year. Tell him about your wedding, Michelle."

"It was long. African weddings are always long. Everyone makes speeches, sings songs, gives gifts. The ceremony alone was two hours, plus it started three hours late."

"That's worse than Kootenay time," Paul says, referring to where he grew up.

"What about the party?" Amy asks. "Lots of dancing?"

"There was some. Not like weddings here, though. It was all over by sundown."

"Really? Sounds lame."

"Hey! That's my wedding you're talking about!"

"Sorry, but it sounds boring."

"Well, it wasn't. You know what, though? Funerals are usually more lively than weddings. People paint their faces and bang on drums and shoot off fireworks for days. We just ate and ate and ate at the one I went to. The whole town shut down. I'd never danced so much in my life."

Amy stays for a while, listening to Paul and Michelle exchange wedding stories. Eventually, she excuses herself. It's a still night, the kind where conversations travel for miles, lingering over faraway houses. She hears the clink of a glass somewhere followed by applause and wonders about the occasion. She walks along the stone path through the herb garden, stopping a few times to look at the moon, almost full but not quite, until she arrives at the greenhouse. Over time, she's grown attached to the wheatgrass, forgetting that it's in constant flux, being planted and then cut down. In her mind, it's the same wheatgrass, day after day, keeping her company, not speaking or judging.

IN MID-JULY, a heat wave sears through the Okanagan Valley, and plants that were once bright with chlorophyll fade to a depleted green. The city issues a water conservation notice and Paul starts talking about the 2003 fires again—the Vesuvian air, how he watered the buildings at night. He and Sharon had been lucky that year, but some of the neighbours were not. On walks, Amy has seen black rectangles where houses once stood.

Matt tells Amy in a letter that things are bad in Toronto, too. *The air conditioner broke last week*, he wrote. *Sometimes I sleep in the bathtub or on the balcony.* Paul wears nothing but his underwear all day, mostly faded boxer briefs, and fans himself with an old newspaper. He gives Amy and Michelle a solar fan for the cabin, but it doesn't help.

"Your boyfriend called again," Michelle says. She's lying on top of her bed in a bathing suit. "And I'm telling you, again. He thinks I'm not giving you the messages. Now he's mean when he calls."

"It's so hot," Amy says. "Every molecule of air is disgusting right now."

"You think this is hot? You should have seen it in—"

Amy cuts her off. "I know. Africa. If I have to hear one more thing about Africa, I swear to God I will throw you out the window."

Michelle's mouth drops open. Amy feels bad but keeps pushing. She's in a fighting mood.

"It gets annoying, you know. Africa this, Africa that. You were barely even there."

"Yeah? Well, you don't need to be a jerk about it." Her voice, though an attempt at sounding fierce, still comes out small.

"You might want to watch it. I'm not kidding about throwing you out the window."

"I think you should leave now," Michelle says.

All at once, there are twenty things Amy wants to tell Michelle, starting with how she thinks Mensah doesn't actually exist and ending with her ridiculous devotion to Paul, a man who interacts with all women in the same generic, flirtatious manner. Instead, she grabs her sleeping bag and pillow and slams the door on the way out.

It takes her a while to fall asleep, lying under the stars at the bottom of the field. Judging by the silence, the neighbourhood dogs are too hot to howl. Her mind drifts to Toronto and she imagines walking along Bloor, past Palmerston where a man plays the harmonica while rattling a tambourine, past the basement bookstores run by sad men who dream of making it big. In the distance, an illuminated orange sign blazes the words *Pizza Pizza* into the night. Her legs stride toward the pulsing sign, almost mechanical. She is drawn to it despite the feelings the sign invokes. Just then, the man from the party appears on the other side of the crosswalk. The hand flashes orange and neither of them moves. When he raises a hand and points in her direction, she realizes he's holding a gun.

Amy pulls herself from the dream and lies in fetal position, panting. There is a metallic sound in the air, like a stream of bullets. After a moment, she realizes it must be Michelle's urine, streaming into the steel chamber pot. Amy closes her eyes, but she doesn't sleep for the rest of the night.

THE NEXT DAY, August 1st, is Michelle's twenty-fourth birthday. It's also the night of Paul's full-moon party, which he warned might get wild. Amy's tired but she still cooks dinner and bakes a cake using fresh carrots from the garden, her version of a truce. They bring the cake to the lower field and eat it with their hands, laughing as crumbs fly from their mouths. "Give me wine!" Michelle says. They've barely had a drink all summer. "Chug! Chug!" Amy chants as Michelle tosses her head back and drinks straight from the bottle.

The tomatoes are bright red and hang in balloon-like clusters. Zucchinis spill across rows and the eggplants hang heavy from their thick, green stalks. At least for a night, the temperature has cooled. It's a much-needed reprieve. In two weeks, Michelle will go back to Vancouver for school and look for a part-time job. There will be more paperwork to do for Mensah and fees to pay with no guarantees. Amy's still not sure what she'll do once the summer's over, but she must decide soon.

"You should move to Africa," Amy says to Michelle. "I mean, you like it so much better there."

Michelle takes the last sip of wine and tosses the bottle aside. Amy waits for a snappy retort but Michelle remains quiet.

"Honestly," Amy continues. "I don't know what you're doing here. I mean, you dress like an African, you talk like an African, and you're married to one. You should be with your people."

Instead of laughing, Michelle covers her face. It takes Amy a moment to realize she's crying. *Shit*, she thinks. *I've gone too far.*

"Come here," she says, putting an arm around Michelle. "I'm sorry. I know you miss it."

Michelle's shoulder is warm against Amy's skin, reminding her how good it feels to be close to another person. Although Matt hugged her at the airport, she didn't hug him back. Not really. She glances at her watch. It would be after midnight in Toronto.

"I can't go back there," Michelle tells Amy.

"Why not?"

"Mensah's family hates me. We got married in a neighbouring village, but of course they found out. They've disowned him. If I can't get him to Canada, I don't know what's going to happen."

"I thought you had a big wedding. All the speeches and stuff?"

Michelle shakes her head. "I wish. It was just me and Mensah and a minister neither of us knew. The whole thing was over in five minutes."

Amy places a hand in the centre of Michelle's back and

spreads her fingers between the vertebrae. She imagines she's sending energy through Michelle's body, healing her somehow. Up at the house, she can hear the beginning of a drum circle and people singing. "Come," she says to Michelle. "Let's go and have a good time and dance and forget about these things for a while." She takes Michelle's hand and they walk there together. Michelle stumbles more than once and Amy realizes she's drunk. When they arrive, Paul lets out a whoop and drapes his arms around their shoulders. His Hawaiian shirt flaps open, exposing the grey hair around his nipples. He steers them to where a group of people sit in a circle, passing out joints.

There are many variations of Paul at the party—men with long hair and beards, most of them with thin, long-haired girlfriends. Some of them have organic farms nearby and one of them, Brian, actually co-owns the land with Paul. His house is next door. When the joint arrives, Amy decides to pass. Michelle takes it, though, and holds the smoke in before exhaling, probably the way someone taught her in high school. When Amy stands up to leave, Michelle follows her but then joins a group of people dancing near the drum circle. She falls seamlessly into their rhythms, her bare feet grinding in the dirt as she twists her hips. *I could never dance like that*, Amy realizes. Even with Matt, there is something clunky about her movements. She lacks grace. Instead of staying at the party, surrounded by strangers, Amy decides to go back to the cabin. Without Michelle, the small space feels comfortable. She lights a candle and takes out her notebook.

Dear Matt, she writes. This time, she has many things to say. She fills one page and then another before she realizes what she's writing is a breakup letter. *Too much has happened*, she writes, trying not the blur the ink with tears. It blurs anyways.

THE NEXT DAY, Amy wakes up to find Michelle's bed empty. It's six o'clock in the morning. She walks up the hill, hoping Michelle got up earlier than usual, though she hadn't heard her return to the cabin. She passes the chicken coop, the tractor shed, the onion patch. No Michelle. At the barn, Amy opens the door and calls her name. She is met by silence. Beside Paul's house, the fire still smoulders and empty bottles litter the veranda. The screen door is open. Amy walks in. *Please don't be here*, she thinks. Someone is sleeping on the couch, but it's not Michelle.

Paul's bedroom is in the hallway, past the kitchen. The door is closed, but she opens it a crack. Paul is lying naked on top of his covers. There is a used condom on the floor. No one appears to be in bed with him.

Amy decides to have breakfast and pay her morning visit to the wheatgrass. Paul swears they've maintained their rapid growth under her tutelage, but she knows it's bullshit. Half the time, she doesn't sing at all. She just sits in there and reads. After the wheatgrass, she checks the cabin and the barn again. Still no Michelle. Harvest has begun and there is much to do, so she digs in silence, filling milk crates with dirt-caked potatoes.

At nine, she decides to check Paul's house again. There is still someone on the couch but they've changed position. She walks toward Paul's room, thinking she'll wake him up and ask him to help look for Michelle. As she approaches, she hears the toilet flush. She pauses outside the bathroom door and waits. The person washes their hands for a very long time. There is silence afterwards. Minutes pass and still there is no movement. Finally, Amy knocks on the door.

"Just a minute," Michelle says.

When she emerges, her hair is stringy and she won't make eye contact with Amy. Unable to remove the judgment from her face, Amy turns and walks back to the field. Michelle follows her like a ghost, not bothering to stop at the cabin and change her clothes. She goes straight to work in a skirt and tank top. Hours pass with no words exchanged. At lunch, Amy makes them sandwiches and they eat near the cabin. On her way to the mailbox where she'll mail her letter to Matt, Paul intercepts her.

"Your boyfriend called. This is what he said: 'If you don't call, I'm flying out there first thing tomorrow.' Buddy means business."

"Thanks," Amy says, walking past without stopping.

The afternoon is hot and the two women spend it in the onion patch, where they'd concentrated most of their weeding efforts all summer. No matter how often they combed over it, the invasive plants always seemed to regenerate. Nonetheless, the onions grew to a decent size. Amy shoves a spade into the ground and lifts, separating roots from soil. Michelle digs with her fingers and pulls. They use their shirts to wipe the sweat from their faces.

"I'm going to call Matt tonight," Amy tells Michelle, hoping for something other than silence.

"Good," Michelle says, still avoiding Amy's gaze.

She wonders if she should ask the question that's been on her mind all morning. *No*, she thinks. *I'll let her tell me if she wants to.* But then she changes her mind. Before speaking, she puts a hand on Michelle's arm. "Last night with Paul," she begins. "Were you conscious of what was happening?"

When Michelle starts to cry, Amy sits close and talks to her the way Matt used to when she was upset, in a voice that sounds like a soft ocean. Michelle's skin is pink from exposure—she didn't put on sunscreen. Amy can feel the heat of it against her skin. In the distance, the ripe eggplants pull toward the ground and the tomatoes stand out, bright red in a sea of green. Amy tries to think of what to say next but none of her ideas have any substance. What she wants is one of Michelle's proverbs. Amy doesn't know the exact phrase in Ghanaian, but she remembers enough of the translation for Michelle to understand. "You can find a worm," she tells her friend. "Even in a ripe pepper."

CONFLICT ZONE

Leslie's porch light illuminates Alex's furled, snow-flecked hair and his thin coat. He's wearing shoes, not boots, and they're completely soaked. Snowflakes pixelate the night, and through that filter, the neighbourhood looks like a grainy photograph of some forgotten past. "Come in," Leslie says, taking his carry-on bag. Alex follows close behind her on the stairs. When they reach the top, she tries to imagine her apartment through his eyes—dirty dishes, overflowing garbage, a bicycle in the middle of the hall.

"Merry Christmas," Alex says, forgetting that she's Jewish. She glances at her watch. 12:23 already.

"You too. It's kind of strange, isn't it? You being here?"

"Yeah," Alex admits. "A bit."

Leslie was surprised by his call, especially since he's supposed to be en route to the Middle East. She imagines him for a moment on a plane with a black ocean below, or maybe by now a blue-blitzed dawn, halfway around the world. At first, when he called and asked to stay at her house because his flight was cancelled, she wanted to say no. For days, she has been hibernating, living off lentils and Sriracha, wearing the same jogging pants in and out of bed, letting her hair become a helmet. But the more Alex talked to her, laughing and joking about the mayhem at the airport and their own recent misfortunes, she felt a surge of emotion, the kind she hadn't felt in months, not since before the trouble started with Kevin.

"Do you want a drink?" Leslie asks Alex, heading for the kitchen while he drops his luggage in her bedroom. She's been drinking too much for weeks, months now.

"May as well," he says.

"I'll make you a strong one. God only knows what you'll be able to get in the Middle East."

His laughter echoes down the hall as she free-pours bourbon into each glass. "Don't worry," he says. "I'll be able to drink in Turkey. I would never intentionally put myself in a position of sobriety."

She puts two ice cubes in each glass and carries the

drinks to the bedroom. She hands one to Alex who is lying on the floor, looking around her bedroom. She did a hasty clean before he came, but there are still dirty clothes in the corner and piles of recently marked exams she was supposed to return to the college.

"So are you going to tell me why you got fired?" he asks.

Leslie and Alex had been colleagues for three years, but Alex suddenly quit teaching just two weeks before the semester started. She hadn't seen him in months until they ran into each other at a party where she found out his wife had left him. They smoked a joint together before he walked Leslie home, holding a broken umbrella to shield them from frozen rain.

"Nope," she says.

Alex makes a pouty face. "How about later? After a few drinks you'll tell me, right?"

"I punched a student," she teases.

"Liar," he says, grinning.

"Okay, it wasn't a punch. I threw a textbook at him. Hit him in the head. Gave him a concussion."

Alex laughs and pokes at her shin with his toe. There's a hole in his sock. *Men*, she thinks. *They can never seem to manage their socks.* She blushes and takes a long drink before placing her glass on the bedside table.

"Right now," she says to Alex, "I'm more interested in how you're feeling. You're going for six months, right?"

"Yep, six to start, but I'll stay longer if things go well."

"How does it feel, trading in your cushy life for a dangerous one?"

Alex pushes his hair, still wet from the snow, back from his face. He narrows his eyes, scrutinizing her.

"I'd hardly call my life cushy," he says.

She knows Alex's background. Rich doctor father and a mother who'd paid for his plane ticket. "Fine, but the Middle East is obviously more dangerous than Toronto. Aren't you scared?"

"Not really. It's not like I'll be on the front lines."

"You don't consider Syria front lines?"

"I'm not going to Syria, Les. Just Turkey."

"Still, near the border, right? Journalists get injured. Kidnapped. Have their heads cut off."

Alex sighs. "I'm getting tired of trying to convince people that won't happen to me. Seriously. I've been through hostile environment training. I'm part of an organization that protects journalists. I have proper safety equipment."

"Like what? Chain mail? An invisible cape?"

Alex frowns. "No. I have a flak jacket."

"Which is?"

"Basically a bulletproof vest."

Leslie feels a stirring at the mention of bullets. "Really? Bulletproof?"

He looks at her quizzically. "Yes. Bulletproof."

She has a sudden flash of Kevin, the time he gagged her with her own panties.

"Can I see it?" she asks.

"No. It's at the bottom of my bag."

"You can't take it out?"

"I could. But not right now. Maybe later we can trade—my bulletproof vest for why you got fired?"

Leslie finishes her drink and wonders if he's going to keep pushing the issue. Maybe she shouldn't have invited him.

"Possibly," she says, crunching on a whiskey-coated ice cube. "But probably not."

I WANT HER, Alex realizes as he watches her from his spot on the floor, triangulated between his backpack and a pile of her clothes. *How long have I wanted her?* They've known each other for a few years. He and Becca were newlyweds at the staff orientation on a humid August day, the kind where the silky lining of your suit jacket sticks to your bare arms. All the new hires stood on the college's front lawn in the noonday heat, posing for a photograph that would go in a staff newsletter no one would read. Leslie was supposedly there, but his first memory of her was from a year later.

"There's this sociology teacher," Becca said one night, exhaling away from Alex. They were sitting on the back porch, smoking a joint. "She's hot. I'd fuck her."

In her early twenties, Becca had experimented with women before deciding that she was mostly into men. Eighty-twenty, she told Alex.

"Yeah?" Alex responded, trying to place Leslie in his mind. He was bad with names and faces.

"I would. I might even let you watch."

The next day at work, Alex went hunting for Leslie's

office. He peered in the window from an angle so she wouldn't notice. That day, she wore a red button-up blouse. He looked at her now, in her own bedroom, wearing a polka-dot dress, bare legs folded to the side. *Becca's right*, he thinks. *She's hot.*

"What do you want to do?" Leslie asks him, pouring two more drinks. "Are you tired?"

"No, I'm wired. Let's talk. Tell me another story, like that one you told me last week. About the gummy worms?"

At the party, after the joint, Alex and Leslie stood by the snack table, eating everything in sight. Leslie began to laugh and wouldn't stop.

"What?" Alex asked.

Finally, when she calmed down, she said, "Once, at a party, a guy asked me to chew up a gummy worm and feed him like a bird."

"What? Why?"

Leslie shrugged. "I don't know. Fetish? Boredom?"

"You'd never met him? He just asked?"

"Yeah, there were a few of us standing around and he said, I've often wondered what it feels like to be a baby bird."

Alex laughed.

"So I did it. I chewed up a worm and when he was ready, I forced it into his mouth with my tongue. Here's the interesting part—I wanted to give him an authentic experience, and I really felt myself becoming a bird. Like, suddenly I imagined myself as a cormorant or something, one of those types with a tiny blue eyes and a mohawk, taking care of a family. It made me want to have children."

"Really? Strange time for maternal instincts. The situation sounds sexy, though."

Leslie gave him a sideways little smile. Shortly after, they'd walked home together. On her doorstep, he hugged her a moment too long.

"I don't have any other wild stories," Leslie responds. "I'm not a wild person."

"Bullshit," Alex says, watching as she takes a cardigan from the floor and drapes it over her knees, avoiding eye contact. She leans against the wall, further from him. For a moment, he lets his mind drift to Becca. *Where is she? Probably at her mother's.* They'd been there together last year. In the car, they'd fought about the usual subject: Alex wanted children, Becca still wasn't sure. She was turning thirty-nine in January.

Two weeks ago, Becca called Alex and asked to meet for coffee. For months, she'd been ignoring him. He wore a nice pair of pants and a dress shirt, just in case.

"I'm pregnant," she said, looking away. "Derek and I are getting married."

Derek was another teacher in the Media Studies Department. The next morning, Alex booked a ticket to Turkey. The earliest he could leave was Christmas Eve.

LESLIE WATCHES ALEX finish another drink and thinks about something he said the week before at the party—teaching is a performance. You size up the class and decide who you want to be based on how people need you to be. There's no such thing as authenticity.

We're not being authentic, she thinks. *We are performing for each other.* At the party last week, Alex's hair had been greasy and he smelled stagnant. A psychic disturbance radiated from him, and she wondered if he could feel hers as well. She hadn't left the house in nearly a week because the last time she took the subway, a little voice in her head said *Jump.* In the mirror, she could see the story of the past three months all over her face. Everyone saw it—colleagues kept asking, "Hey, are you okay?"

"It's just a tough semester," she lied. "Difficult students."

The problem, though, was Kevin. Kevin, her former lover, a man she met on the internet. It didn't take long to schedule their first date. Kevin quickly developed a sense of what might excite her, like putting a hand up her skirt while on the subway or flogging her with a dirty rope he found at Harbourfront. For months, he came to her house twice a week. Then one day he didn't show up. She texted once, twice, thirty times. He never responded. Once, she called—no voicemail.

On the Tuesday after Labour Day, she walked into her sociology class wearing a blazer and dress pants. She set down her briefcase and took off the blazer, hanging it on the back of a chair. She wrote her name, Dr. Leslie Krone, on the board. Below, she listed her contact information and office hours. When she turned to face the class, she saw Kevin sitting in the second row.

"You can't be here," she told him after class.

"No?" Kevin responded. "Last I checked, it's a free country."

"I don't want to see you back here."

"I can't take the class any other time because of my work schedule," he said, holding her gaze.

She never did find out if he was enrolled in a program or if he'd just signed up for the thrill. His status was marked Independent, which could mean anything. Every week, he came to class. He called her *ma'am* and raised his hand to ask questions. She couldn't teach with him in the room—not the way she usually did. *Please*, she prayed every Tuesday when she woke up. *Make him go away.*

Alex finishes another drink and moves from his spot on the floor to the bed, close to Leslie. She steals a glance at his watch—3:25 AM.

"You know why I want to go to the Middle East?" he says. "Aside from needing to get away from teaching?" She doesn't answer but he continues anyway. "I want to report on the rebel infighting. It's pretty interesting. How many groups do you think are fighting in Syria right now?"

"Is that a trick question?"

"No. How many?"

After a pause, she says, "Three? Maybe four?"

"In a way you're right because of alliances. But actual groups? Probably a thousand."

Leslie's eyes widen. "Seriously? That many?"

He nods. "It's hard to know for sure, but there are definitely hundreds. The whole thing's a quagmire. Like, you have ISIL fighting the Al-Nusra Front, who is fighting the Syrian Armed Forces. Most of them get weapons from the same places. Actually, no. A lot of weapons get made."

"What kind of weapons?" Leslie asks, suddenly interested.

Alex laughs. "You're so morbid. They make bombs, obviously. But anyone can make a bomb. We could make one now if you have fertilizer and kerosene."

"We could bomb Becca's apartment," she says.

Becca lives in a house now, he wants to say, but realizes if Leslie doesn't know she's moved in with Derek, something has happened between the two women. He has no idea what the house looks like inside. When he stopped by earlier that week to pick up some books that had accidentally gotten packed with hers, she made him stand on the doorstep.

Alex rolls off the bed and crawls across the floor to his backpack. He undoes the clasp and begins hauling out gear—shirts, fatigues, mosquito net, boxers, headlamp, toiletries, a jar of Nutella, first-aid kit, notebooks—

"Alex, what is that?" Leslie points to a large pink crystal. The shape reminds her of a sea anemone with its flat bottom and tendril-like prisms.

"My mom is one of those New Age people," he says, passing it to her. "It's supposed to give me courage. You can have it."

"You can't give away something like this," Leslie says. "You'll jinx yourself." She holds the crystal to the light and watches it change colours depending on how she turns it.

Eventually, Alex passes her a garment. It looks like something a grandfather might wear on a fishing trip.

"What is this?" she asks.

"The bulletproof vest."

"*This?*"

"It needs the protective plates, but yes." He roots through his clothes, unwraps the plates, and inserts them into different pockets.

"Wanna try it on?"

"Yes!"

Leslie notices Alex noticing a flash of her panties as she stands up. She is still as he guides her arms into the vest, conscious of its weight on her shoulders, his hand moving from her navel to sternum, past her breasts when he pulls the zipper. She has another flashback of Kevin, a night in August when he tied her to a chair.

Alex stands back and observes Leslie. "You look good," he says.

"If you had a gun," she tells him, "I'd let you shoot me."

She watches his reaction, amused by how he tries to hide behind a neutral expression. *People are always so afraid of their feelings.*

"If you get me a knife," he responds, momentarily letting his fascination show, "I'll stab you."

Leslie goes to the kitchen before he can change his mind. *This behaviour,* her therapist recently told her. *Your attraction to violence needs to stop.* She agrees, yet she feels a wave of euphoria when she takes a knife from the drawer and presses her finger to the tip. *Am I crazy?*

she wonders. *Probably.* The numbers on the stove's clock flip to 4:06 AM. She doesn't feel at all tired.

"How do you want to do this?" she asks Alex, back in the bedroom.

"I'm thinking we should be careful. Do a kind of trial run?"

"No, that's boring. Just stab me. Make it real."

Alex laughs nervously. "Whatever you say."

While he stands with the knife, mentally preparing himself, Leslie thinks of the night Kevin tackled her in the hallway and cut off her dress with scissors. That was the best time. She watches Alex and wonders if she should keep her eyes open or closed when he drives in the knife. Open, she decides, so she can watch his face. How will he react? Part of her assumes aroused, the other part thinks ashamed.

"Okay," she says, locking eyes with him. "I'm ready."

ALEX STUDIES HER torso and considers where to put the knife. *There are weaknesses*, he thinks. *I know all of them.* Leslie is watching him too intently and he feels under a microscope. He closes his eyes to avoid her gaze. *How do I want to frame this?* he wonders. Becca floats into his mind again, goddamn her. Becca in their old kitchen, hair pinned at the nape of her neck, blouse tucked into a pencil skirt; she'd made an effort to look good that day.

"Where were you?" he asked. She'd come home after midnight, saying she'd been out with Brigitte. He knew it wasn't true.

"Liar," he said. She ignored him.

"Slut," he said.

She turned around, face etched with hate.

"Fuck you," she said.

He'd been so in love with her cruelty, the way they brought out the worst in each other. In Leslie's bedroom, he imagines it's Becca standing in front of him. *Number one rule*, he imagines saying. *Take a shower before you go home.* He tightens his grip on the knife and thinks about where to stab. The gut where he felt her betrayal the most, or the heart? Gut or heart. Heart or gut.

Both, he decides.

"Go," Leslie says.

Alex feels the blue veins rise on his hand as he grips the knife even tighter. He thinks of something she said the night she kicked him out: *Your aspirations are tepid. They're like weak tea.*

He could put the knife into the centre of her body and slit open her stomach. Gut her like an animal. He thinks about her stomach for a moment, how on Christmas morning last year, while she slept, he'd placed a hand on her belly and imagined there was a child growing there. He'd always wanted a little boy.

Alex opens his eyes. Leslie's are still closed and she's standing there with her arms open, almost in rapture. He puts the knife down.

"Sorry," he says. "I can't do this."

Leslie gives him a curious glance before taking off the vest. "You'd make a lousy criminal," she jokes. Alex sits on her bed and holds out his glass for another drink. She fills it and then her own. Alex feels the bourbon move through him, calming his nerves, but he can still feel the tension in his hands and jaw. What scares him most is how for a moment, with his eyes closed, the knife felt okay in his hand. Hurting someone seemed like a pretty easy thing to do.

"We should sleep," Leslie says, stretching out in the bed. Lately, she's been going to bed early and getting up late.

"Not yet," Alex says. "You owe me a story."

"About what?"

"About how you got fired."

"Why do you care so much?"

"Because I can't figure out why anyone would fire someone like you."

Leslie turns onto her side and looks at Alex. She remembers so clearly when they first met at the staff orientation—she immediately knew she wanted him in her life. She reaches for his hand and holds it while she tells him what happened with Kevin. The only other person who knows anything is Becca—earlier in the semester, they went for a drink together and Leslie decided to confide. She realized her mistake as soon as Becca called her dynamic with Kevin "sick."

"You have to report him," she said to Leslie, cutting her off before she could finish explaining the context.

"For what? He hasn't actually done anything. It's the potential for him to do something that makes me nervous."

"He's blackmailing you. If you don't give him good grades or play by his rules, he'll show the photos to the wrong people."

"He's not blackmailing me. He does all the assignments, and they're better than everyone else's."

"Why are you defending him, Leslie? You should have reported him the very first day. I can't believe you've put yourself in this situation. God."

Leslie didn't respond. In a way, Becca was right.

"Whatever you do," Becca said, "make sure you don't sleep with him. You'll get your ass fired."

What Leslie hadn't explained to Becca is that, over time, her anxiety shifted focus. At first, she worried every time Kevin put up his hand in class, wondering what he might say. But he never said anything wrong. He just answered questions with articulate responses. She could feel him watching her as she lectured and drew diagrams on the board. Over time, she came to enjoy that sensation of being watched.

One afternoon in November, Kevin showed up at her office.

"What do you want?" she asked.

"You know," he responded.

She let him in. He closed the door and kissed her. He pushed her back onto the desk and spread her legs. "Shhhh," she warned as he bit a hole in her pantyhose. They didn't speak, didn't make noise the whole time. He did everything slow but deep so the furniture wouldn't shift and give them away. When they were done, she offered her scarf so he could wipe himself clean. It was the last time she ever saw him.

"What happened, exactly?" Alex asks. "Did anyone question you? Was there an investigation?"

"Nothing. I can't be a hundred percent sure of what happened. All I know is that Kevin stopped coming to class. There was a departmental meeting later that week where the coordinator mentioned reports of inappropriate student-teacher relations without being specific. Becca hasn't spoken to me since. I'm almost certain she reported me."

No, Alex wants to interject, but he stops himself. After eight years together, three of which she'd been cheating, it's still there. His pathetic loyalty. "What makes you think that?" Alex finally asks.

"Just a feeling I get, plus I saw her near my office when Kevin left. She gave me a look."

Alex feels the dread in his stomach. He knows exactly what look Leslie is referring to. "But it might've been that guy. Kevin?"

"It could have been him, but my intuition says Becca. Whatever the case, when the time came to assign classes, the coordinator told me there'd been an unexpected decrease in enrolment and there wouldn't be any work for me."

"That's bullshit," Alex says.

"I know, but I'm on contract. They can do what they want. I'm fucked. My career is over."

"Hold on a sec here. No one even talked to you about the situation, so there isn't anything on your record.

You could easily get another job. Most of the time, people don't even call your references."

"I know, I know. But I just . . . I guess I'm scared."

"Of what? The college probably wants to let the situation settle. I bet they'll hire you back in the fall."

"No way," she says. "I'm never going back there."

"You shouldn't. You're too good for that place. And what happened isn't so bad," he adds. "Male teachers sleep with students all the time. I'm not saying it's good. I'm just saying it happens."

"Still," she says, turning off the bedside lamp. "I wish it didn't happen to me."

Alex checks his watch—5:37 AM. He'll need to leave by eight because of the holiday bus schedule. For a while, he lays in bed with his eyes open, half-tempted to start something with Leslie. But he doesn't want her to think it's for the wrong reasons. Alex drifts for another hour, until the horizon begins to lighten, thinking about Gaziantep, the city where he'll share a house with a few other independent journalists. Finally, around seven thirty, he decides to get up. As he quietly packs his bag, he thinks about what Becca said, that his aspirations are tepid. He imagines himself making connections in Kilis and eventually crossing into Syria where he'll write articles about the rebel infighting. *I'm going to break stories*, he realizes. *Be all over the international news. My name will be everywhere.*

He thinks about waking Leslie but decides against it. She looks so peaceful, sleeping with her head turned to where Alex used to be.

AT SOME POINT in the night, Leslie felt Alex let go of her hand. Now, she reaches for it but is surprised to find the bed empty. She opens her eyes and checks her phone. It's 8:27 AM. Two empty glasses sit on the bedside table. Outside the window, loose snowflakes shimmer as they hang suspended in the air. The storm is over, but Toronto has become a white planet in its wake. *Today*, she decides, *I'm going to do laundry.* She looks to where Alex's clothes and first-aid kit and bulletproof vest were strewn about and suddenly remembers him moving around the room, the slight rustling, the final click as he fastened his backpack. None of it remains now except the strange pink crystal from his mother, sitting on her desk, its prism-like facets catching the early morning light.

CENTRE OF THE UNIVERSE

STUPID RHYMES WITH CUPID

The first time we had a conversation, I was in grade 10 and you were in grade 12. Right before Christmas, your band played at the school talent show and I couldn't stop laughing because you spat water into the crowd and nailed the principal's left breast, an act that earned you a one-week suspension. When you came back in January, I cornered you in the hall. "Guess what?" I said. "I had a dream about you last night. You had three legs!" That dream didn't actually happen, but it certainly got your attention. We talked at length about the possible mechanics of such a body—you said walking would be more of a trot and I said a three-legged person would probably drag the middle one like it didn't exist. We both agreed pants would be difficult.

We didn't talk again until the summer. Your band had a new album and the launch party was at the gravel pits out on Theatre Road, a name that doesn't make sense because there's no theatre anywhere. A man with a purple mohawk sold home-recorded cassettes out of a cardboard box and told anyone who didn't buy one to go the fuck home. During the show, the generators made more noise than your guitar, but no one cared because at least something was happening in town for once. At the end of the first set, the bassist dumped gas over a pile of pallets and lit them on fire. You stood against the backdrop of flames drinking Canadian Club straight from the bottle and told people you wanted to be a porn star.

"Imagine, sex all the time and you even get paid."

The statement secretly made me cringe, but I said, "Yeah, yeah, totally." I blushed, because I was a virgin at the time. Turns out you were, too. I should have known. Who else would brag about wanting to be a porn star?

That fall, I was back in school but you were gone. Not only had you graduated, you'd moved from Cranbrook to Vancouver so you could start a "real" band and write books until one day some publisher opened their eyes and said "Holy fuck, Nathan Matlock is a cool asssss mother-fucking writer." Then you would be famous.

I KNOW HOW TO APPRECIATE BEAUTY
I KNOW WHAT'S BEAUTIFUL

I was in grade 11 when you came back from Vancouver. I saw you one afternoon by the clock tower downtown, on a day that made me happy to be alive—burnt wood smell in the air, a crispness over everything.

"Hey!" you shouted. "Three-legged girl!"

Your hair was longer but you kept the sides close-shaved like a real punk.

"Come for coffee?" you asked.

I shrugged like I didn't care and followed you to a nearby café. As we stacked creamers to impossible heights, you told me about all the cool friends you'd made in Vancouver, like Sid the draft dodger who lived in an underground city, and Malcolm who kept bees on his roof. You also told me about the time you got high on mushrooms and told people in the streets that *life is a bad remake of a cult classic based on a screenplay adapted from an incoherent novella.* The cops found you ranting at the corner of Hastings and Columbia and took you to a hospital. You kept yelling on the gurney because the acoustics tripped you out. I bet you sounded like an eagle when you screamed that night.

While living in the big city, you worked at a recycling plant where employees wore masks to keep the mould away. *Mounds of dead carton post-liquid and blue with right-angles meshed into abstraction* is how you described your work environment. At night you listened to community radio, sometimes in languages you didn't understand,

and called in requests that never got played. Sometimes you found great things in the recycling, like fur coats and antique weathervanes, that you later sold at flea markets.

Once, you found a story in the heap. It was about a dragonfly that travelled to places where people lived in grey and brought colour to their lives. In the story, a woman who'd lost her husband stood at the sink crying because instead of two dirty plates there was only one. Soon enough, the dragonfly flitted past the window, bringing colour with each palpitation. Eventually the trees changed to green, the flowers to orange, and the sun's reflection flamed white-gold. The sad person couldn't help but cheer up.

You read me the story while I drank my third coffee. What a voice you had. Just like a radio announcer, and I always wondered why you never became one. "Wow," I said when you were done. "That's really good. Really."

You folded the paper up small and slid it across the table and told me I could borrow the story for a while. Eventually, the paper wore thin and the ink bled purple along the folds because I carried it everywhere. In later years, when we could no longer bear to speak to each other, I threw it away because I was convinced you no longer believed in beauty.

I wish I still had it.

DO YOU REMEMBER THE FIRST TIME WE KISSED
We became friends immediately. Most days, you drove me home from school via the junkyard where you collected scrap metal and wires for your various art installations. Sometimes we drove to Kimberley where they had a

yodelling cuckoo clock. Local kids had started sneaking up the back of it at night to change the yodelling tape. You never knew what you'd get—death metal, Malcolm X, the Jabberwocky. One night, you sent me up the clock to put in one of your band's tapes, but a security guard came after us before I could finish the deed.

In December, we started our own gang. The mission was social justice and our main goal was to protect the town from the new Wal-Mart. People were going crazy spending their money and some local stores had gone out of business. We spent a lot of time drinking coffee at the Husky, you and I, discussing the trickiness of promoting local sustainability while smashing capitalism. Under the bright restaurant lights, we made hundreds of posters that said things like VIOLENCE IS A FAILURE OF THE IMAGINATION and YOUTH AGAINST FASCISM and ONE DAY THE POOR WILL HAVE NOTHING LEFT TO EAT BUT THE RICH and the one you liked most—LOVE YOUR FAMILY, KILL YOUR TV.

Our relationship had been strictly platonic from the beginning, but that changed Easter Sunday. My parents were mad at dinner because I ate fast and refused to say grace. You barely ate anything because you were a vegetarian. Since we understood each other so well, we tended to skip nonessential words when speaking, meaning no one else could understand our conversations. It drove my parents crazy. After dinner, my mother brought out a Jell-O and pineapple dessert. When you mentioned how gelatin is really made with horse hooves, we were asked to leave.

The road was blackened with ice and we fishtailed three times on the way to the Husky. After several coffees, we hit the streets and taped mean posters to stores we didn't like and left love notes for the ones we did. In the doorway of the only independent grocery store left in town, we stood close and strategized how to keep it in business aside from bombing the WalMart. Later, we walked to Rotary Park. You put down your scarf and we sat on it by the cenotaph, inventing life stories for the soldiers.

"What do you think about the fact that we're all going to die someday?" I asked.

You thought death was something a person would mentally participate in until the absolute end, at which point the still-active mind would enter a new chamber of consciousness.

I said that didn't make sense at all.

We agreed to disagree.

Driving back to my parents' house, you were unusually quiet. I asked what was wrong and you said you thought I should be your girlfriend.

"But you're my best friend," I said.

You seemed unsure about how to respond to that. The uncertainty looked good on you and suddenly I wondered if us being just friends was a mistake. Without warning, I pulled over in front of the Alliance Church and said, "Kiss me right now so we'll know." Conscious of your coffee breath, you unwrapped a piece of gum and gave me half. We counted to three.

It didn't feel like kissing a friend. Not at all.

It was like turning on a switch: everything was the same but different. We still drove around in your van listening to thrashy punk groups no one had ever heard of and drank lots of coffee at the Husky, but instead of hugging at the end of the night, we would kiss. Our relationship felt more complete that way. We tried taking off our clothes to bring our intimacy to a new level, but each attempt ended with us discussing how it felt staged, like we were trying to live out fantasies that had been canonized by popular culture. *Are we asexual?* we wondered. *Is there something wrong with us?* Eventually we stopped asking questions and just accepted our way of being with each other.

One night in July, the day's heat still radiated from the sidewalk long after dark, so we drove out to Monroe Lake to cool down. It was mid-week and there was no one around except us. There was a rope swing on the shore and you could practically fly to the middle of the lake if you ran fast enough. Along the banks, the black pines stitched land to sky and I wanted to stay there forever. The two of us ran and jumped and floated for hours until our skin wrinkled, then we made up old person names for ourselves—Gertrude and Hank. Our splashes that night sounded like the only thing in the universe.

In the van driving home, you said something I will never forget:

"I bet if we both wrote a book it would be the same."

HONESTY. NOW. IS WINNING.

In September, I started grade 12. Most of my friends had already graduated and I knew it was going to be a year of awkward loneliness. You said we could meet for lunch every day, except your boss at the pizza place switched you to day shift. I ate most of my lunches in an empty classroom.

A week after school started, a guy named Joe showed up in homeroom, which was a big deal because no one new ever came to town. People just left. For the longest time, all I knew was that Joe came from the Okanagan and once spent a summer painting apartments in New York. We sat at the same table in visual arts. Joe didn't really talk to anybody so I didn't talk to him either, but we shared a comfortable silence while we worked. Sometimes we admired each other's paintings.

Visual arts was in last period and I often stayed after class to work on projects. Most of the time I had the place to myself, but Joe stayed once to finish a painting of the Staten Island dump.

"Fresh Kills," he said. "That's what it's called, and did you know the garbage is piled higher than the Statue of Liberty?" I admitted I did not. My painting was a trash can full of flowers—lilies with bent stems, bleached daisies against metallic grey. I'd seen it on the way to school earlier that week and thought it was the most beautiful thing.

Joe and I kept working on our trash until it got dark. As Joe layered pastels over charcoal, he told me about New York in the summertime—the steaming rats in the alleys and break-dancers at Union Square.

"I've never really been anywhere," I told Joe.

"You'll go places," he said.

The conviction in his voice and his certainty that I would not live and die in the town where I was born made me cry. Tears led to comfort, which led to a kiss, and before I knew it, we were in the supply closet taking our clothes off.

I wish I could say I felt guilty, but I didn't. Lying to you was easier than I ever imagined. "Yearbook club today," I said with a shrug. "Call you later? I've joined the swim team."

You could not hide the hurt, though you tried. Over time, you stopped asking questions. I started to feel dissociated, like I was watching a movie of myself drinking coffee and having long conversations with you. It got to the point where I didn't feel like I was kissing you. My lips were just moving. I did not want my lips to just be moving with you.

I wish I could remember how we broke up. Was it in the park? In your van? How long did we not talk? Nothing from that period of my life is clear, except that I felt horrible once our lives parted ways.

Joe and I didn't last long. Our connection was never anything but physical. Eventually, he stopped coming to class and then school altogether. Someone said he moved to Kelowna. Another said he got a job at the pulp mill.

On Valentine's Day, you left a note in my mailbox that said THE HEART IS A CLENCHED FIST ENTRUSTED TO A NONEXISTENT IDEA. A few weeks later, I saw you walking in Rotary Park. "The heart is not a clenched fist!" I yelled.

You stopped in front of the cenotaph, and when I caught up, you told me I had been your dragonfly—your world was grey without me. We soon went back to driving around together and talking on the phone and drinking coffee at the Husky, but there was no kissing. I just couldn't. Not after what I'd done with Joe.

After graduation, I left town because I'd been accepted to a French immersion program. There was no way of knowing at the time, but we would never live in the same place again. I stayed in Quebec after the summer because I wanted to have a fabulous life and knew that would never happen in our town. You quit your pizza delivery job in October and moved back to Vancouver for the same reason. For the next ten years, you oscillated between town and city, never sure where you wanted to be.

I SUPPOSE THERE IS NO "GOOD" TIME TO TELL YOU I STILL LOVE YOU.

We hadn't been in contact for years when you wrote this in an email. I lived in Montreal with a boyfriend who wanted to marry me. I didn't want to write you back until I knew what to say. I waited too long. Eventually, you sent a message that said, THE DISRUPTIVE AMBIENCE OF THE IRRECONCILABLE SPREADS LIKE SUNLIGHT AND OIL. GOODBYE.

I know very little about your life after this moment. Because you refused to speak to me, I had to make up a life for you in Vancouver. Your apartments were never nice and I'm sorry I couldn't have dreamed up something better.

One was a small studio above a flower shop on Pender Street. You wrote your first novel there, on a typewriter at your kitchen table. The window faced a brick building with crazy tenants who threw knives at each other. I see you going to three different coffee shops, depending on your mood: one is a diner where they serve cherry pie that is gluey from being in the fridge too long. You never eat the pie. You just sit with your notebook and drink coffee and write. The other two coffee shops are independent, run by artists like yourself. I see you at a microphone in front of a hushed crowd. I see a lot of respect and friends who love you.

A few years ago, my mother sent me a clipping from the local newspaper. You'd just had your first book published. I cried when I read it because we still lived thousands of kilometres apart. What I wanted most was to have coffee with you and maybe pull over somewhere afterwards to see if we still felt the same. Instead, I did nothing.

The last time I saw you was in September. I was back in town for my mother's funeral—she'd dropped dead in WalMart from a heart attack. Feeling nostalgic and too sad to cook, I took my father's truck and drove down to the pizza place where you used to work. Imagine my surprise when I found you behind the counter. Nothing about your appearance had changed, but somehow you didn't look the same at all.

"Hey," I said.

You pretended you didn't know me.

ONE LAST TIME

LAST FEBRUARY, I DECIDED TO go to Mexico because someone I barely knew died. A twenty-three-year-old musician, friend of a friend from Vancouver who I met at a party once. I thought she was so beautiful, but in a simple way that made some people look at her as plain. After I heard about her passing, how she died in her sleep for no discernible reason, I found myself watching her one and only music video on repeat. I memorized the earrings she wore, the mole on her chin, her curly hair, the space between her teeth. Knowing she was no longer in the world felt like the worst thing and I couldn't figure out why. I guess I saw her potential to be great but knew that instead, she'd end up being forgotten.

I left three weeks later, on Valentine's Day. The gate was populated mostly with businessmen and couples leaving for romantic holidays. I wondered how they would classify me, if they even registered my existence, and decided based on their gazes, either on their phones or on each other, that they did not. The plane left at three and I tried to hold back the nausea, ignore the high-pitched pressure in my ears as we gained altitude, tried not to think about how scared I felt, losing gravity, regretting the decision altogether.

There was a stopover in Dallas at sunset, an event everyone watched through the terminal window. The sky was all hot coals, clouds on fire, and the entire American Air crew, pilot and all, sat in a row beside me, immobilized, silent. Planes mapped the horizon, landing, hovering; the sky looked magnified and I couldn't help but think of my mother, working at an airport all those years. She spent most of her life in the terminal café, admiring the mountains, earning a meagre wage to raise me properly, mistake that I was. Before my flight, I stopped to kiss her goodbye and she snuck a sandwich into my carry-on. *I love you*, I texted before the connecting flight left Dallas. *So much*, she wrote back.

As we flew through the night, I flipped through my guidebook to Mexico City, a used copy, dog-eared and marked according to someone else's sensibilities. I tried to guess what kind of people they had been based on the marks and symbols—probably young backpackers. They never stayed anywhere expensive. Neither would I. Below, the full moon reflected on the water. Could the fish beneath it feel the glow?

City lights soon blanketed the landscape and a quagmire of boulevards mapped the city's sprawl. When the wheels hit the runway, the passengers around me had that look on their faces—home. We docked in the terminal and I followed the Mexicans until we were separated into two lines, one for residents and then me, not quite alone but almost. You were there, Alessandra, all tattooed and gorgeous. We talked our way through the customs line and I wondered if you were flirting, hoped you weren't just being a friendly traveller. It's hard to tell with some women. We took a taxi together, traversing the city, and you placed a hand on my thigh. At the hostel, even though I booked my own room, I spent the night in yours, wondering how someone I barely knew could feel so familiar.

The next day, we wandered. *Huevos rancheros* and *café con leche* on the hostel rooftop with a view of a smoggy, massive downtown, then *plazas, mercados, museos*, and a narrow alley with old printing presses where you had someone design a card that said SWEETHEART BE MINE. The man misspelled SWEETHEART even though you told him twice and he eyed us with curiosity, simultaneously aroused and disapproving. Over dinner, fish tacos in Zona Rosa, we agreed that we'd met a hundred times before—we were peasants in Constantinople, goddesses on a Grecian island. We'd drowned together during World War Two.

On the way back to the hostel, too late at night for unchaperoned women, we met a man chain-smoking outside his apartment. He invited us inside to see his *galería*, a living room crowded with paintings and blank canvases and low-burning candles that made the art seem curated instead of haphazard. You could tell by the colours and geometrics that most of them were from the eighties, images of social justice dreams and the national debt crisis. The man, though he wasn't the artist, felt connected to the art. He was moved by our interest, the way we stood in front of each canvas for so long, and he wanted to give us a painting.

"No," you told him in Spanish. "We don't even live here." "*Por favor, bellísimas*," he insisted, pulling one down called *Sueños Solitarios*, a fugue of black and red. We carried the enormous painting through the streets, shifting our weight and laughing, ignoring the looks of everyone, including the hostel's night guard, as we carried it to our room.

I wonder if it's still there.

The next morning, I woke up first, excited by the very fact that you exist. I texted my mother and said, *I met someone. You would love her.* She texted back, *Hopefully one day I will.* When I could no longer be good and let you sleep, I slid my hand across your stomach, knowing you'd wake up and make love to me, once, twice. We eventually showered and took the subway to the Terminal del Norte where we caught a bus to Teotihuacan, the Aztec pyramids north of the city. Vendors filed through the narrow aisles of the bus and tried to sell us things like cookbooks and tiny screwdrivers and love potions. We ate homemade ice cream out of small plastic bags and listened to Manu Chao as the city sprawl thinned to grasslands outside the window. I rested my head against you and tried not to think about Wednesday, your departure for Mazunte, how I'd be alone in the city and what that might feel like. At the pyramids, we took selfies like we planned the vacation together, and I couldn't help but wonder if you did the same thing with other women, if it was easy for you on the road, if you erased the photos when you arrived in the next town.

We were starving by the time we returned, but most restaurants near the hostel were closed because it was Sunday. A man on the street told us to go to Plaza Garibaldi, which wasn't far. He didn't tell us the place would be full of mariachis, absolutely full, a cacophony of trumpets and small guitars, men with round bellies belting out *"Aye Mi Amor!"* wearing dapper clothing with many metal clasps. There was a twenty-piece band on stage and a nonstop smoke machine clouding up the plaza. We kept ordering margaritas and a guy from the kitchen came out because he saw your sleeve from a distance. *"Donde?"* he kept asking, pointing at the tattoos. Where did you get them? You waved him off, saying, *"No aqui. En Italia,"* hoping you were saying Italy right. He told you he had ugly tattoos. *"Feo,"* he said, voice laden with disgust. We reassured him that they couldn't be so bad until he lifted his shirt to expose an array of truly hideous shapes, faded and stretched beyond recognition.

What I didn't know that night, drinking margaritas and kissing you, my three-day girlfriend, best I've ever had, was that I would wake up the next day and find out my mother, my sweet mother, my forever friend and confidante, had a heart attack while we were eating enchiladas.

I received the news early in the morning. The sun had already penetrated the Mexico City fog, all bright orange behind long garlands of cloud. You sat up in bed, hand in my hand while I spoke on the phone. My mother's landlord regretfully informed me her chances of survival were less than five percent. She'd collapsed in the laundromat parking lot. Luckily, someone noticed her body, even though it was late at night. Had it happened at home, she would have died alone.

You helped me get dressed, looping my arms through one of your sleeveless blouses while I cried. You booked me a flight. You said everything was going to be all right and kept your arm around me. We had breakfast on the patio, a hasty affair of weak hot chocolate and cornflakes, before you took me to the airport in a taxi.

"We'll meet again," you promised, kissing my face, my neck. "We'll be violinists in Spain, lovers on the moon."

"Come with me," I said.

You walked as far as you could, all the way to the security gate, and kissed me one last time.

In Dallas, there wasn't much to see except a man waiting for his children who lived in Miami. I found out that he flew them out for two weeks every month. As they came through the gate, eleven and nine years old, I could see the trauma all over their faces, the custody battle, the con-fusion. They reluctantly hugged their father, not making eye contact. *At least you have a father*, I wanted to say. *At least you have someone.* On the plane, memories rushed in—the time me and Mom rented a car and went to Vancouver Island, all the way to Tofino. We had a picnic under a blue September sky, ate avocados, and buried the seeds in a grassy area so that one day we'd go back and have trees to remember us. That day, we swam in our clothes, thrashing in the waves, weighed down by pant legs while our shirts ballooned in the water.

I remembered my nineteenth birthday party at her trailer, and how we listened to "Runaround Sue" and danced in the kitchen half-drunk on cider. Lobsters we bought from a roadside truck boiled in a huge pot. "Lobsters!" we laughed, watching the shells turn pink. "What are they doing here?" For dinner, we sucked the tiny strings of meat from the shell, all salty and decadent, and you told me that one day I would have it all.

I landed at the Abbotsford airport and tried not to look at the café while I waited for my luggage. As I drove toward Hope, the setting sun filled my rental car with golden light. Irrigation sprinklers ticked in wide arcs, leaving tiny rainbows over the parched grass. The entire valley was so dry I feared it would disappear in a roar of flames if someone lit a match. Eventually, I arrived at my destination and parked by intensive care. I walked through the double doors, into a crowded waiting room until a nurse brought me to where my mother lay unconscious.

There, I spent three days unable to get enough air into my lungs as I watched her, not even fifty years old with a brain that would never work again.

What I remember most about our last day together was how the nurse let me wash her hair. She didn't say *one last time*, but the words were there anyways. They have this no-rinse dry-shampoo cap you can put on an unconscious person's head, so the person doesn't have to be moved. They can just sit comfortably while being massaged. I tried every technique—pressure points, shiatsu, massaging her third eye, hoping I could bring her back to life. I talked to her for an hour, working on her neck and temples, realizing how bending down all those years in the café must have destroyed her muscles. I told her about Mexico and about you, Alessandra, the paintings, the people, the food, all the gold in the churches, how with you I felt something people might call love. It took years for me to find it again.

Finally, the nurse came. She removed the cap from my mother's head and readjusted the bed. She pressed some buttons on the machines and wrote notes in her chart. Afterwards, the nurse gently placed a hand on my arm and asked if I needed anything. I told her a coffee might be good. While she was gone, I held my mother's hand and hugged her tight. Already, her scent was starting to fade.

SEPTEMBER

I LEFT ESTERHAZY EARLY ON A Tuesday. Most of the kids at the group home slept while I packed my belongings once and for all, but some of the older ones stood in the driveway and waved through their haze of envy—I was getting out. My car, a rusted Honda someone sold me for a dollar, would likely fall apart before Manitoba, but I didn't care. I was on a mission. Fuelled by internet success stories, I had decided I was going to find my mother.

The afternoon was all Kenny Rogers and stealing gas, zooming past rail lines and fluorescent canola fields. "Ruby, don't take your love to town!" I screamed out the window as I drove east, my fake twang echoing off grain elevators. Portage la Prairie, Winnipeg, Lake of the Woods—I held my breath as I entered Ontario for the first time. That night, the sunset over Lake Superior nearly destroyed me. The bright pink sky burst into the car and seemed to hug me. It felt like love and I couldn't stop crying.

Three days later, I arrived at the Quebec border. BONJOUR, the sign said. Farmland gave way to derelict warehouses and a knot of highways converged at Montreal's city limits. Side-winding past old factories turned into lofts, I was confronted by the sudden realness of a place I'd only dreamed of. Everything was so French— the billboards, the stop signs, the radio ballads. I'd never seen such tall buildings. The sun's reflection flashed across a thousand windows and I couldn't help but imagine my mother, out there somewhere, shielding her eyes from the blaze.

SLEEPING IN THE car was only supposed to last a few days, but money went quick and there was Pete—a sometime train hopper from Tennessee, living in a converted school bus at the corner of Duluth and Esplanade. His banjo music flooded the intersection where I waited for a pedestrian to cross, not sure where I was going or what I was looking for. Maybe it was him all along. I followed the sound until I saw his bare feet dangling from the blue roof.

"Hey," I shouted.

The music stopped and Pete's face appeared, hair furled under a pageboy cap. He looked like a chimney sweep.

"Hey-o," he said back, tossing down a rope ladder.

That night, he told me about hopping trains all over North America, the ocean views, and how you could go south but not north in Mexico because the banditos would slit your throat. "The bus is okay," he said, "but I miss the sway of the train, the grate of the tracks."

I told him I'd come looking for Marie Tremblay, my mother, a woman who decided early on she did not want me. Social services had put me in contact with a lady who finds lost parents, and she'd followed my mother's trail out east. Still, there was no guarantee she still lived here. No guarantee she was even alive, for that matter, but I was willing to try anything.

I made a list of 164 Tremblays who might be my mother. Every morning, after Pete rode his too-small bicycle to the Old Port where he shoved screwdrivers up his nose and stapled things to his chest for pocket change, I made calls from the Dairy Queen pay phone. The flashing neon cone gave me courage. Across the parking lot, people bought discounted parfaits with coupons printed on the backs of grocery receipts. The smell of hot fudge and waffle cones nearly drove me crazy, I wanted them so bad. Instead, I ate dry Ichiban and stolen chocolate bars. "*Salut*," I said to anyone who answered the phone. "*Parlez-vous Anglais?*" They probably thought I was some degenerate, trying to scam them out of their life savings. Sometimes I said French things I'd copied from Google—"*Je cherche ma mère. Est-ce que c'est toi?*" No one understood my accent. Men with names like Marcel Tremblay seemed sad about my situation and women like Maude wished me all the luck in the world. Madeleine started to cry—she'd given up a child, too.

"I think of him every day," she wept through the phone.

I told her to look for him.

"I already did," she said. "He won't return my calls."

"One day he'll change his mind," I assured her. "You'll see. Just be patient."

PETE AND I met at six every night behind the dumpsters at Jean-Talon market. Neither of us had money for real groceries, but a lot of the stuff vendors threw out looked better than what we had at the group home. Primal instincts flared as soon as I got between those metal walls and I felt like a hunter-gatherer, wrangling zucchinis and bell peppers. Punks from other city parks went there, too. They looked so cool with their dogs and patched clothing. Some were squeegee kids, others were train hoppers. I couldn't tell the difference, but Pete could.

"Dirt versus oil," he said. "Look at their knees."

I learned how to cook kale and make eggplant taste like steak. "No more Hamburger Helper for you!" Pete said. We dined in his rooftop garden among seedlings that sprouted from ice cream pails. After dinner, we'd split up the chores: whoever wasn't on dish duty had to get water. I hated getting water. The park bathroom was always disgusting with wads of wet toilet paper on the floor and a lingering diaper smell. The small sinks meant I had to dump mugs of water into a bucket over and over again just to get enough water for dishes and the garden. After chores, Pete and I swapped stories about our days and I told him about Marie Tremblay.

"I bet she's a singer," I said. "A dancer, a drifter, a fire-eater."

"We'll start our own road show," Pete said.

"Cool. What's my act?"

"Snake charmer?"

"Ew! I hate snakes."

"You'd be great," he said. "You have the courage and patience, and you're already a charmer."

The compliment burned my cheeks.

Every night, people played soccer in the park and sang loud French songs on picnic blankets full of decadent food. We drank Belle Gueule on the roof and sang our own songs. At the end of the night, we tossed the empty cans down to a bottle collector named Bernard. It was like an arcade game with his bag wide open as we placed bets on the rim shots—breakfast, beer money, mostly water-fetching duty. Pete hated it, too. Eventually, we bought paper plates.

BY THE END of July, I hadn't found my mother. I'd hoped it would be easier, that I'd walk into a labyrinth of Tremblays who knew each other or that the universe would just bring her to me. Sometimes, I envisioned us passing on the street—we'd immediately know we belonged to each other. I looked at everyone, studied their hair and skin. No one in that city looked like me.

Every day I made calls, but they all led to the same place—nowhere. At night, I circled my finger on the dwindling list and waited for a sign, a clue, anything that might lead me to her.

"I don't know what to do," I told Pete.

He reached across the dirty plates and took my list. He held it against his chest. Eyes closed with the stapler wandering, he circled once, twice. *Tack!* No matter how many times he did it, I still winced whenever the metal hit skin.

"There," he said.

The staple had marked 3970 Esplanade. Just up the street.

"Genius!" I yelled, scrambling down the rope ladder. I hit the ground running, sandals a-clack.

"No, no, you tumbleweed!" Pete shouted after me. "Come back and finish your wine!" Suddenly I was athletic, sprinting down the avenue. Voices in a language still strange to me rose like steam from backyard patios. I counted down the addresses, rehearsed what to say if my mother happened to be on the stoop, happened to be getting out of a car—did she have other children? Seventeen years since she'd left me at a church wrapped in a pair of sweatpants, birth certificate under my chin. Why did I want this?

In the end, it didn't matter. I was out of breath, standing in front of an empty lot. Instead of my mother's house, there were bulldozer tracks. Nothing left there but a pile of bricks and mortar.

AS THE SUMMER rambled on, the city became crowded with tourists who flocked to Mont-Royal for pictures with the statue, a stone angel with a quiet, Eastern salute. Pete loved their money, but I hated everything about them, especially their happiness. Whenever I saw them sashaying by on family outings, I wanted to throw rocks. By the end of July, temperatures flew to incredible heights and I coped by eating ice cream in the shade. Some days, the air felt so thick you could taste it.

I made Pete tell me over and over about the trains, the squats, the places he'd been.

"Don't get all romantic," he said. "You get cold, someone tries to cut your face, you smell bad, and you're half-starving most of the time."

"But you loved it," I said.

"Yes," he confirmed.

He watered the garden and sang songs and let me staple money to his chest. Sometimes we drew extra zeros and pretended we were rich. He tried to teach me to stick a screwdriver up my nose so we could busk together, but I could never get past the nostril.

One night in August, I tried to kiss him.

"Jailbait!" he shouted.

"I'm seventeen!"

"Exactly."

He was twenty-five. That night, after he went to bed, I took the rest of the wine and lay in the back seat of my car, wishing I had money for more booze. Sometimes, all I wanted to do was wreck myself. Just drink myself blind and punch holes in things. I could become the person everyone expected me to be. It was too hot to sleep, even with the windows open, and my thoughts kept returning to Marie Tremblay. Where was she? Awake or sleeping? In a bed or on a bender? An ambulance raced into the hotel parking lot and I thought, *That could be her. Maybe she wrecked herself.* I wiped the sweat from my forehead and took off my shorts. They were sticking to my thighs. Pete had a fan—I could hear its hypnotic whir from a distance.

I knocked on Pete's window. He parted the curtains, eyed my tank top and panties.

"Nice try, kid." He closed the curtains.

No choice but to get dressed and go to the Esso. I browsed for a while, enjoying the refrigerated air, and I stole a bag of ice on the way out. By morning, I was hugging the waterlogged remains under a tree, wondering how much longer I could survive. That's when I saw Bernard, the bottle man without his bottle bag, wandering around shirtless. I barely recognized him in daylight. His torso was a litany of old sailor tattoos. A thick paste collected at the corners of his mouth and lines of perspiration marked his neck. He looked at me and said, "*Il ne te reste pas beaucoup de temps.*"

I understood what he meant—time was running out.

I had the Tremblay list in my hand, dog-eared and full of handwritten notes. I passed it to Bernard. "Help me," I said.

He took the paper and stared. Even his wrists were sweating. Whatever drugs he'd taken were vigorously circulating through his body. The list sailed out of his hand and fell on the grass.

"*Il ne te reste pas beaucoup de temps*," he repeated before walking away.

I picked up the list. One of Bernard's thumbprints had marked the address 13, 2E AVENUE in Verdun. I hadn't been there yet and no one ever answered when I called. Thirteen—it was August 13th—surely a sign? I put the list in my pocket and ran to Sherbrooke metro station. The man in the booth counted my loose change and handed me a map. He circled the stop I needed: De l'Église, on the green line. Only then did I realize how little I'd seen of the city all summer.

From De l'Église station, I walked down Wellington Street. Cafés doubled as doughnut shops and men in track pants had loud conversations on shabby *terrasses*. In between bargain stores and shoe warehouses, there were bistros with expensive entrées. Something about the neighbourhood felt fake. People looked as if they should either be on game shows or in the hospital. I followed Wellington up to 2e Avenue, a street overrun by garage sales with ugly trinkets and outdated electronics. *A gift for my mother*, I thought, picking up an antique dinner bell. "*Touche pas!*" a hag screamed from the doorstep. I put down the bell and kept walking. As I counted down the addresses, people stared out windows through translucent curtains blown wild by oscillating fans. They all seemed to look right through me.

Apartment 13 was on the ground floor. The curtains

were closed so I decided to sit on the curb and wait. Snippets of conversation sailed from nearby balconies, too fast for me to understand. Questions I asked myself: *What would life have been like here? Would I have been a French person? Would my name still be Katie?* It wasn't long before I heard a door open behind me. A voice said, "*Petite puce, dépêche-toi!*" I didn't need to see the woman. There was no way she was my mother. Her voice sounded too young, too carefree.

For the rest of August I scoured the city, visiting one Tremblay after another. On Rose-de-Lima she was black, on Sherbrooke she was in her sixties. The M. Tremblay at Cadillac was a man; so was the one on Bourbonnière. It was Marie-Claude who lived on Pie-IX and Marie-France on Hutchison. Day after day, I crossed addresses off the list until there were no Tremblays left to find. Then it was September.

PETE HAD TO leave on Labour Day—something about joining a travelling freak show and needing to see a man in Chicago about it. The night before his departure, after he went to bed, I sat in my car and cut myself, something I hadn't done in years. The streetlight's reflection came straight through the windshield and I put a pillow over my head to block it. Still, the all-night buses fluming on Park Avenue and a man screaming "I've been fucked by Christ!" kept me awake until dawn.

In the morning, I helped Pete ferry things down from the roof. I dismantled the small table where we'd eaten dinner and played cards while Pete brought down the garden a bucket at a time. Most of the plants had dried out or been picked clean.

"Take the peas," he said. They were still going strong.

"Let me kiss you," I said.

"Fine. But no tongue."

I held his face against mine as long as I could.

"Cheater!"

Before he left, he placed his pageboy cap on my head.

"You look beautiful," he said, adjusting it.

I stood beside the pea plant and watched him drive away. Then I sat under a tree and cried. The skies were steel-wool grey that morning and the wind scooped garbage and flung it around the park. An empty chip bag flew by and I thought, *My life is trash.* I tried going for a walk but everything reminded me of Pete—the *dépanneur* where we bought beer, the smoked-meat place where we shared a sandwich whenever Pete made extra money, the corner where I'd first heard his banjo. I knew I couldn't stay in Montreal by myself, but I didn't want to go back to Esterhazy. It wasn't home. I needed money, though, and I knew exactly how to get it there because I knew all the wrong people. I unlocked the car and sat in the passenger seat, head against the steering wheel. That's when I noticed a paper on the dashboard: Pete's phone number. WAIT A FEW YEARS, he wrote. WE'LL MAKE UP FOR LOST TIME.

I'd gambled all my cassettes away to Pete, so I made up hobo songs as I drove west through the city. With the sun in the rear-view mirror, I said goodbye to the parking space that had been my home and the dumpsters that had kept me alive. The skyline faded behind me and the sign at the border said AU REVOIR.

"Goodbye, Tremblays," I said, thinking of all 164 of them. "Goodbye, unknown mother."

The day passed; Ontario passed. I stole coffee at gas stations and drank until I felt I might explode from anxiety. Every town brought me closer to Esterhazy, the group home, the life I'd hoped to leave behind. I unfolded my Tremblay list and scanned it at the side of the road. Had I given up too soon? What if someone had misunderstood? It wasn't too late to go back. Another possibility—maybe I had called her. Maybe my own mother had heard my story and said, no. Sorry.

I pulled over a few times to nap but mostly drove for two days. By Wednesday, the land was all range roads and prairie fields once again. Farmhouses flickered in and out of focus and canola smeared the ground like bright fingerpaint. I crossed the border between Manitoba and Saskatchewan, marked only by a wooden sign. When the gas gauge dipped below the fill line, I realized I had no money left to fill the tank. The light came on and I coasted into the nearest village. Pete's hat was on the dashboard—his power radiated through every fibre. I put it on and studied my reflection. Orphan-like, yes, but Pete was right. I looked beautiful.

I ate a few peas, shell and all, while I thought about what to do. Eventually, I decided I should at least get out of the car. Across the parking lot, there was a family restaurant. I walked over, wishing my pockets weren't empty. The sandwich board boasted of homemade pies and my mouth started to water in a bad way. I opened the door and stood in the entrance, admiring the red leather banquet seats and ice cream machine. The people inside looked so nice, they made me want to stay.

MONTERRICO

LEIGH AND JUSTIN MET AT the airport after taking the SkyTrain from opposite directions through a torrent of frozen rain. They hadn't seen each other in six months.

"*Hola, señorita,*" Justin said, handing her the ticket. During the flight, he talked nonstop about everything that had happened since the summer while she listened and nodded politely. Afterwards, they boarded an old school bus that trawled down a pockmarked highway, en route to Guatemala's coastal lowlands. Justin made up nonsense lyrics to go with the stomping tuba music blasting from a radio duct-taped to the dashboard. He danced in his chair and tried to get Leigh to join. She wouldn't. No one sat near them unless they had to.

"Bet they're afraid they'll catch gringo," Justin said.

Monterrico was the last stop on the route. They arrived late at night. Justin was already standing in the aisle, cigarette pack in hand, before the bus reached a full stop. He elbowed his way to the door, chanting "*Disculpe! Disculpe!*" Leigh sighed and collected everything he'd left behind—his iPod, a magazine, snacks he'd bought from a child in the airport parking lot. She was the last to leave the bus.

"Wanna drag?" Justin asked, offering his cigarette.

"I quit."

"Really? When?"

"After we broke up."

"Good girl," he said, blowing smoke in her face.

"Fuck off," Leigh said, slapping the cigarette out of his hand. Justin laughed.

They waited beside the bus for their luggage. On the roof, the driver manoeuvred through webs of twine and lowered down suitcases, a box of watermelons, a crate of unruly chickens, and a smashed-up motorcycle. It took three men and a pulley system to successfully lower the motorcycle. Once on the ground, the owner strapped the chickens to the back and pushed the bike away. One by one, people collected their bags and disappeared into the night.

"What now?" Leigh asked.

Justin shrugged. They walked down the street, past boarded windows and locked gates. Nothing seemed to be going on anywhere. Eventually they spotted a sign that said SERVICIOS PARA TURISTAS. On the porch, a flit of moths charged and receded from a naked bulb. A boy sat alone at a table inside the hut. Leigh guessed he was seven or eight years old; Justin thought younger. The boy pushed a toy car with a pencil until it crashed off the table, then he crouched on the floor and drove it up the leg.

"*Hola*," Justin said through the screen door.

The boy looked up.

"We're looking for somewhere to camp," Leigh said, making a tent shape with her hands.

The child put the toy in his pocket and motioned for Leigh and Justin to follow him. They meandered through side streets until the roads turned to sand. In courtyards, dying coals glowed orange in firepits. A dog with knotted fur lay on the road, either sleeping or dead. Finally, the boy stopped and unlatched a gate. Justin did a sweep with his flashlight—an outdoor kitchen and a small hut. Pots and pans with scorched bottoms hung from rusty nails by the sink. A fish carcass lay nearby, black with flies.

"There's no camping on the beach?" Leigh asked.

The boy shook his head.

"How much for the night?" Justin asked. "*Cuánto cuesta?*"

The boy shrugged. "*No sé.*"

Justin scowled. "This little fucker's gonna try and hose us. *Cuánto cuesta?*" he repeated.

The boy pointed to the hut. "*Mi padre*," he said. His father was sleeping.

"Let it go," Leigh said. "I'm tired."

"Fine. But we're not paying more than thirty quetzals, that's for damn sure."

Leigh held the flashlight while Justin set up their tent. A NEST FOR THE LOVEBIRDS, his mother had written in the Christmas card. He snapped the poles into place and drove the pegs into the ground. Once the tent was set up, he lit another cigarette.

"Be there in a sec," he told her.

Leigh could feel his eyes on her ass as she crawled through the vestibule. There was still trail mix in the tent seams from when they'd last gone camping together. She laughed, remembering how angry he'd been when he caught her snacking in the tent. "Bears, Leigh," he'd said. "Jesus."

After he finished his cigarette, Justin entered the tent and took off his shirt. He'd lost weight, though he'd always been thin. Cross-legged, nozzle in mouth, he blew until his mattress was taut. Afterwards, he took off his pants and lay on top of his sleeping bag. Leigh turned so she wouldn't have to see him. The smell of Old Spice deodorant wafted from his armpits and it reminded her of the night they met, when Leigh had been out at a bar on Commercial Drive and heard him crowing to a group of friends about selling a painting for ten thousand dollars. He was dressed in black, but not in a morose way.

"You," she said, leaning across the table. "Come over here."

"No," he said. His friends laughed. Leigh turned away, embarrassed.

Five minutes later, the waitress brought her a drink.

"From the man in black," she said.

That night, Justin stayed at her apartment. She fell asleep in the crook of his Old Spice scented arm and they spent the whole next day together, walking around Commercial Drive like they owned it. The process of moving in together happened quickly, organically, and there was talk of marriage early on.

After they broke up, Leigh deconstructed the relationship from every possible angle but could never pinpoint when, exactly, he'd fallen out of love with her. There were no signs. He just woke up one morning and started packing.

"It's not you," he said. "It's relationships."

By noon, he had his clothes in garbage bags. She watched him spiral down the stairs and hail a cab in the street. His energy lingered in the apartment for a long time. She kept finding things—his socks in her drawer, a stick of cinnamon gum in the couch cushions. Sometimes at night, she hallucinated his off-key singing, the sound of a paintbrush.

When he called on Christmas Day, they hadn't spoken in months.

"Didn't I tell you to leave me alone?" she said.

"What? Leigh! Hear me out!"

She sat cross-legged on the floor, twirling the phone cord as he explained the tickets to Guatemala, a combined

Christmas and anniversary gift. He'd bought them during a seat sale right before he dumped her. They were nonrefundable.

"Obviously circumstances have changed," Leigh said before hanging up.

He called back immediately.

"Come on! Don't be a spoilsport."

In the end, it was a word that changed her mind: spoilsport. What nerve he had.

THE NEXT MORNING, Leigh woke up early, roused by the shock of warm weather. A radio blared in the courtyard. "*Dios, iglesia!*" cried an evangelist. "*Mi salvador!*" a crowd shouted back. Justin pawed in Leigh's direction, mumbled something incoherent, and went back to sleep.

Leigh sat up and looked out the tent window. A middle-aged man stood in the courtyard, wearing only underwear. He tipped a red bucket over his head, closing his eyes as the water splashed against his body and soaked the dirt below. When he refilled the bucket, a cloud of flies rose from the sink. Water spilled over the rim as he pulled the band of his underwear and lathered in a slow, circular motion. Leigh moved from the window so he wouldn't notice her watching. Beside her, Justin continued to sleep. When they were still a couple, Leigh often awoke with an errant strand of his hair in her mouth. "Men shouldn't have long hair," she'd often teased. "Especially at your age." He was twenty-six. She would be twenty-nine that summer.

Salt and sandalwood—that's how it tasted.

Justin eventually rolled over and opened his eyes. "Good morning, *señorita*," he said to Leigh. He lit a cigarette in the vestibule and lay on his stomach as he smoked, exposing the thin, stretched backside of his underwear.

Leigh tossed him a pair of shorts. He put them on and went looking for the property owner to settle camping fees. The man from the courtyard was now dressed in jeans and a collared shirt. Justin sauntered over and shook his hand. The man sized up Justin's hair and naked chest while they circled each other, practising the ancient art of negotiation. Justin stood his ground until the man agreed to his price.

"Dude wanted thirty-five quetzals but I got him down to twenty-five!" he said as they walked into town. He'd bargained lower than four dollars a night.

"Cheapskate," Leigh said.

They meandered through side streets, retracing their route from the night before. In courtyards, laundry hung from makeshift lines and children in school uniforms stared as they passed. "*Gringa*," one said, pointing at Leigh's blonde hair. "No," Justin corrected. "*Canadiense*." At the only store they could find, Leigh filled a bag with fruit. Justin rooted through the fridge, looking for cold beer. It was all warm. He uncapped two bottles outside the store and handed one to Leigh.

"Cheers," he said.

Leigh took a long sip. The alcohol went straight to her head and made everything sharp and strange. A bus trawled down the road while a man hung out the side door, shouting "*Guate! Guate!*" He seemed like a character in a play. The bus, bright green and blue, had cursive lettering on the side that said JESUS GUIA MI CAMINO.

"Hey," Justin pointed down the road. The sign from the night before: SERVICIOS PARA TURISTAS. Leigh hadn't recognized where they were. The same boy was drinking coffee on the porch.

"Aren't you too young for coffee?" Leigh asked. His name, she remembered, was Joselito.

"Buddy, come to the beach!" Justin said, giving the child a high-five. "Just for a bit. There aren't any *turistas* who need *servicios* right now, are there?"

"*No puedo,*" Joselito said.

"Poor kid," Leigh murmured. Justin gave Joselito another high-five before they left. They walked down the street until the beach came into view. Ten-foot swells rose against a flat blue sky and each break sounded like a string of earthquakes. Jagged black dunes carved by the powerful surf gleamed in the morning sun. At the end of the road, an empty lifeguard chair stood tall, weathered by salt and wind. There were no life preservers along the shore. Justin drained the last of his beer and tossed the bottle aside. He kicked off his sandals and crow-hopped across the burning sand.

"Geronimo!" He charged into the ocean and stood with his fists out, waiting for a wave. *Idiot*, Leigh thought. She watched a wave crest and curl before pulling Justin's body underwater. Milky froth hissed and spread across the ocean's surface. Leigh scanned the water for a head, an arm, anything. Another wave rose against the horizon. Still he didn't resurface.

"Justin!" she cried. The soles of her feet burned as she ran toward the water. Immediately, the undertow sucked at her ankles and water rose to her knees. She was about to dive in when Justin washed up beside her, shorts half off.

He hiked them up and charged back in.

Leigh fought the undertow and clawed her way back to shore. She spread her towel on the sand and lay on her side, exhausted. When Justin had proposed a beach vacation, burning sand and killer waves weren't exactly what she'd imagined. No one else was swimming. Aside from a lone figure in the distance, no one was even at the beach. Leigh could understand why. She flipped through a magazine and watched Justin. Before long, the figure on the beach came into focus. It was Joselito, still dressed in long pants and a heavy cotton shirt. Leigh waved him over. Justin noticed and came to shore.

"Hey, buddy!" He ruffled the child's hair with a wet hand. "You must be hot. Don't you want to swim?"

Joselito shook his head.

"Right—no bathing suit. Just take off your pants! No one cares." He put his fingers into Joselito's belt loops and tugged. The pants were too big and they slid past his hips. Joselito stood in his Spider-Man underwear, stunned. He put a hand over his crotch and stared at Justin. Leigh was about to ask if he was okay when he began to giggle. He took off his shirt and ran down the beach, letting out high-pitched shrieks. Justin chased the boy for a while and then opened another beer. He stood ankle-deep near the shore, looking out at the horizon. Joselito joined him there and took his hand. From that angle, they looked like father and son.

Leigh watched as a massive wave rolled in, sending forth a barrage of foam. Suddenly, the water was up to Joselito's waist. He screamed, yanked his hand from Justin's and ran back to his clothes on the shore.

"Are you okay?" Leigh asked.

Joselito looked at her with dilated pupils as he forced his pants over his wet underwear.

"Are you okay?" she asked again.

He grabbed his shirt and ran.

"That was stupid," Leigh scolded as she walked with Justin to town, looking for Joselito.

"He said he wanted to swim!" Justin responded, offended.

When they found him back at the tourist information booth, playing with his toy car, Justin shot Leigh an infuriating told-you-so look. Nonetheless, they picked up more beer and spent the afternoon at the beach. Later, when they arrived back at Manuel's, they found someone had moved their tent. In its place were two hammocks filled with young girls. "*Peluca*," one said to Justin, pointing at his long hair. The girls shrieked with delight when he flopped into one of the hammocks.

Leigh filled a bucket to rinse the salt from her body. The water rushed over her skin and pooled at her feet. She leaned over the sink to refill the bucket and noticed a reflection in one of the pots. Manuel was watching from the yard.

Leigh hung up her wet towel and went to change in the tent. When she emerged wearing a sundress, a woman was in the kitchen, making tortillas. Probably Manuel's wife, though she looked much younger than him. The woman flattened circles of dough between her hands and placed the tortillas on a rack over a low-burning fire. Her T-shirt barely covered her protruding belly. *Pregnant*, Leigh thought. Her body remembered it well.

She offered the woman her hand. "*Me llamas Leigh*," she said.

"*Maria. Encantada.*"

Leigh told Maria in broken Spanish that she and Justin had spent the afternoon at the beach. Maria slapped the dough between her hands as she spoke. Her response came too fast for Leigh to understand.

"Justin, come here," Leigh called. He raised his head from the hammock, hair in sloppy braids. He looked like a rag doll. Maria smiled as Justin approached, taking clown-like steps as he walked. She spoke to Justin the same way she'd spoken to Leigh, quickly, but Justin was able to understand most of what she said.

"She hasn't been to the beach in years," he reported. "It's too dangerous."

"*Uno de mis hijos se ahogó. Tenía solamente doce años.*"

"I think she said a boy drowned twelve years ago."

"*Las olas te pueden romper el cuello. Se prudente, pueden matarte.*" Maria made a wringing gesture with her hands.

"She says we need to be careful. We could break our necks."

Leigh studied Maria's face, the way her jaw set as she spoke through clenched teeth. She thought of Joselito that morning, his soaked underwear clinging to his skin.

"*Tendremos cuidado*," Justin assured Maria. To Leigh, he said, "I promised her we'd be careful."

After sundown, they went back to the beach. Leigh turned her face to the night sky, buried her hands in the sand, felt her sunburn glow. It was February 20th. Had she and Justin stayed together, it would have been their anniversary. They passed a bottle of beer between them and Leigh wondered if she should ask for a cigarette. She wasn't used to travelling as a nonsmoker.

"You're actually good with kids," she said to Justin. "I mean, aside from almost drowning Joselito."

"Hey! I told you. It was his idea, not mine."

"He really likes you."

"Yeah? Good, I guess."

"You looked like father and son at the beach."

Justin laughed. "Leigh. The kid is brown."

"I just mean . . . the way you were together."

"I'd be a shitty dad," Justin said, lighting a cigarette.

"Maybe not."

Justin took a long drag and exhaled up to the stars. They were both quiet for a while. Whitecaps glinted under the half-moon's frown and ocean spray fizzled above the waves. Leigh could feel the alcohol moving through her body, dulling the edges of old wounds, and she reached for Justin's cigarette.

"No," he said, gently placing her hand back in her lap.

She looked at him, sitting there in his shorts and T-shirt as if he'd never belonged anywhere else. He hadn't changed at all in all their months apart. Justin met her gaze and let a handful of sand funnel through his fingers onto her leg. So many times he'd done just that on lazy beach afternoons in Vancouver and elsewhere. When he reached the hem of her skirt, he stopped and put his hand there.

She let it stay.

"*ALABA EL SEÑOR! Mi salvador!*"

The next morning, Leigh unlocked her body from Justin's and searched for her clothes. Her sundress was wedged underneath Justin's mattress. Outside, the laundry line creaked as Maria and the neighbour hung out clothes and spouted prayers at each other. It was hard to tell if they were engaged in a friendly debate or an age-old feud. Leigh pulled on her wrinkled dress and unzipped the tent. On the way to the outhouse, she passed the hut where Maria and Manuel slept with their children. The television blared without an audience. Inside, there were five beds and no windows. She climbed the steps to the outhouse and hovered over the seatless, concrete toilet. Her urine slapped against the sand below.

This is poverty, she thought.

When she returned to the tent, Justin was awake and dressed. "Let's eat," he said, taking her hand. In the early days, it was what she missed most—walking with him, being seen in public. They were the kind of couple people noticed. As they walked into town, she realized something had changed: the length of their steps, maybe the pacing. They were no longer in sync.

"Here?" Justin asked in front of a small cantina on a side street.

Leigh shrugged. A Coca-Cola fridge hummed mechanically while a game show blasted somewhere behind the cash register. A triangle of sun cut through the otherwise dark room. "*Huevos rancheros para dos*," Justin said to the waitress, holding up two fingers. He picked up a table and moved it into the light. He took an ashtray from the counter and lit a cigarette.

"Don't," Leigh said when he flopped into a chair.

"Don't what?"

"Don't act like we're a couple."

Justin cocked his head.

"You just ordered my food," she said. "That's a couple thing."

"Oh, I see. I can un-order your food if you'd like."

"I'm just saying."

"You were acting pretty couple-y last night . . ." Justin raised his eyebrows.

"That was a mistake."

"Leigh! Come on."

"No," she said.

Justin considered her response as he exhaled. He narrowed his cheeks and blew a few smoke rings.

"Spoilsport," he said.

THAT AFTERNOON, MONTERRICO changed. Techno music bleated down the road and buses spat diesel as the weekend crowd rolled into town. Laughter and catcalls filled the streets and derelict buildings suddenly became bars and restaurants. By late afternoon, the main street had become a parking lot. "*Gringos! Venga!*" a woman said, hanging a bottle of rum out a bus window. She poured a shot into Justin's mouth. Large groups of people milled about town, talking loud with drinks in their hands. Most of them were drunk students from Guatemala City, but a few were teachers. Leigh kept running into one named Alvaro. Even though he wore aviator glasses, she could see his eyes following her whenever they crossed paths.

Somewhere between the margaritas and *cervezas*, ferrying between party buses, Leigh lost track of Justin. She'd last seen him being dragged off by two young women in bikinis. Leigh had been jealous, not of the girls, but of Justin's ability to have real conversations. She, on the other hand, remained in the background, mostly answering questions with *sí*. Eventually, she stumbled out of the bus and hobbled through the crowds barefoot, looking for Justin.

"*Chica!*" a male voice said. Leigh turned to confront the voice. It was Alvaro. Unlike everyone else in town, he didn't seem drunk. He offered his arm to her.

"I'm okay," she said.

Alvaro made a *tsk tsk* sound. "You *Americanas*. So independent."

"Canadian," she corrected.

On the main street, people sold beer out of milk crates in their front yards. No one thought to sell water. "Wait," Leigh said to Alvaro when they passed a store. It was next to where Joselito worked. Alvaro waited for her outside. The clerk stood at the counter with his shirt unbuttoned, sweating while people drank cold beer in line. Some dropped money on the counter and left instead of waiting. Leigh, knowing the price of water, added her quetzals to the pile.

She found Alvaro talking to Joselito in front of the tourist information booth. "I was just asking your friend how I might get a nice *Canadiense* girl to walk with me on the beach," he said.

"And?"

"Your friend thinks I must ask your boyfriend. It is true?"

"He's not my boyfriend."

"Good," Alvaro said. "Then you have no reason to not walk on the beach."

"I don't have any shoes," she said.

Before she could protest, Alvaro disappeared into the store and came out with sandals a few minutes later. "See?" he said. "*No problemo.*"

They were plastic and lime green, but they fit well. She and Alvaro walked toward the beach, past impromptu bars that blasted Top 40 music through speakers fed by long extension cords. Near the lifeguard chair, players lunged at each other in a heated soccer match. A few people waded near the shore. Leigh did a quick sweep for Justin but didn't spot him anywhere.

"Do you come to Monterrico often?" Leigh asked Alvaro.

He pushed back his sunglasses and squinted at the surf. "Sometimes," he said. "My students need someone *sabio* to make sure they do not get too stupid with drink."

"You're a teacher, right?"

"Yes, now I am teacher. But first, I was lawyer."

"Really? Wow!"

"Yes, wow. But you must understand, to be lawyer here is nothing. All the justice is . . . how do you say? When people pay money to police? In Spanish, we say *soborno*."

"Bribery?"

"Yes. Bribery. It is all the time happening in Guatemala. Here, lawyer is not really lawyer. It is more like *marioneta*." Alvaro danced his hand through the air like a puppet master. "And you?" he asked. "Do you come here often?"

Leigh laughed. "No."

She had begun to think of the beach as her own even though she'd never gone further than where the village ended. They walked until the music faded. Alvaro took off his shoes and rolled up his jeans. Houses expanded in size the further they walked and their designs became more grandiose, sophisticated.

"You see there?" Alvaro pointed ahead. "It is the home of Efraín Recinos."

"Who?" Leigh asked.

"Efraín Recinos, a very good artist. The style, it is surreal like Salvador Dalí. The colours are like Picasso."

The home of Efraín Recinos was immaculately white. Submarine windows lined the second floor and marble staircases connected each floor. Leigh closed her eyes and imagined living in a house like that, watching the sea from above. Every morning, a palette of cutting sky and dark ocean.

"It's beautiful," she said.

The day was starting to wane. The late afternoon sun hovered at the edge of a sky with no clouds. After a stretch of empty beach, there was another mansion. Two guard dogs paced behind a security gate, snapping their teeth. Alvaro suggested they turn back. As they walked, he asked Leigh about her life in Vancouver. She told him about one of her jobs, designing puppets for a theatre company. "*Marionetas*," she said, mimicking his earlier hand gestures.

"You would like where I am living," he said. "In the *centro historico*, by the theatres."

"Do you ever go?" Leigh asked.

Alvaro didn't answer. He was looking down the beach. Leigh followed his gaze and saw Justin. Even from a distance, it was clear he was drunk and looking for trouble.

"Maybe you should go," Leigh said.

"You said he is not your boyfriend."

"No, but he's not good with other men. I think you should go."

"I see," Alvaro said, hesitant. He kissed Leigh's cheek

before walking ahead and promised to find her later that night. Alvaro nodded a greeting to Justin as he passed, but Justin ignored him.

"Who's that grease bag?" Justin asked when he reached Leigh.

She shoved him. He fell back, arms akimbo. Once he regained balance, he draped an arm around Leigh's sunburnt shoulders. "Ouch," she said, removing her arm. "That hurts."

Justin grinned. "Feisty," he said. "That's why I love you."

She pretended she didn't hear and kept walking. Soon enough, he fell into step beside her and tried to put his arm around her once again. She dodged it. Everything about the scene was so familiar. For Justin, she realized, time had not passed. In his mind, she was still his girlfriend.

THAT NIGHT, THE transformations continued. Boats were kicked out of storage sheds and the spaces became dance clubs. Students from Guatemala City filed through the streets, dressed like they were in the capital's *Zona Viva*. Leigh felt underdressed in shorts and a tank top. She and Justin lounged on a blanket beside the sea, taking a time out from drinking. She even closed her eyes and had a small nap, but once the clubs opened, it was impossible to sleep. Leigh watched as a posse of girls wearing tight skirts paraded down the beach in V formation, hips swaying. They walked lopsided, heels sinking in the sand. Leigh knew before they arrived what their mission was: Justin.

"*Hola*," one said. "*Te gusta bailar?*"

Justin looked at Leigh and then at the girl. "Just one song," he said.

She watched him go into a club with the skinny little fawn. Leigh focused her gaze on the ocean, appreciating its agitated beauty. Fifteen minutes passed, then twenty. After a half hour, she took a walk, looking through open doors where lovestruck couples danced close under strobe lights, lost in some illusion of permanence. She circled behind the clubs, remembering how she and Justin used to paint walls with the sweat of their backs. When she found him, the girl's skirt was up so high Leigh could see the trim of her panties.

Leigh went back to where they'd been sitting and shook the sand out of the blanket. She folded it over her arm and began to walk back to Manuel's, thinking how fucked up her life had been after Justin left. She'd skipped work, refused food, and did something unheard of: cried. Friends tried to reason with her. "Get over it," they'd said. "He's a jerk."

"I know," she'd wailed.

What bothered her most was his indifference, his infuriatingly flat emotional register. Nothing seemed to matter to him. They'd only been together six months when she found out she was pregnant. Not that she wanted to keep it, but she still felt something when the blue line surfaced on the test. She told Justin immediately.

His response was a groan. "We're broke," he'd said. "What are we supposed to feed it? Puppets? Paint?"

They'd both laughed even though it wasn't funny.

At least he'd taken the day off work to bring her to the clinic. She'd give him that. And he didn't dump her right away. No, he stuck around for another six months.

THE RUMBLE OF breaking waves pulsed beneath Leigh's feet as she walked along the beach. On the road to Manuel's, two young teenagers sat on a concrete block passing a beer between them. Leigh smelled food somewhere and longed for it. She followed the trail and ended up at a restaurant close to Maria and Manuel's. The night before, it had been nothing but a dark courtyard.

"*Qué bueno!*" a voice said. Alvaro was there, face lit by candlelight. Leigh pulled up a plastic chair, surprised to find him alone. An empty cocktail glass suggested someone else had been there earlier but left. There was a small, handwritten menu with three items: PESCADO FRITO, POLLO ENCEBOLLADO, TACOS AL PASTOR.

"You are very lucky," Alvaro said. "The woman who lives here, Renata, is the very best cook. Maybe the best in Guatemala. You will see. All the food here is . . . *magnífica.*"

"Good," Leigh said. "I could use something *magnífica* right now."

Alvaro pushed his beer across the table. "Here," he said. "This will do the trick." Leigh laughed and took a drink. Alvaro leaned back in his chair and stretched out his feet. Leigh did the same. Alvaro glanced at her painted toenails and the lime-green sandals. "Your shoes," he said.

"Where did they take you today? Other than the home of Efraín Recinos."

"Nowhere, really," she said. "Just to the clubs. It's not really my scene."

"You understand now why I am here where the music is not loud and there is drink and good food," Alvaro said.

"Absolutely. Cheers to that," she said, holding up an invisible bottle. Alvaro laughed and raised his bottle to her empty hand. He signalled for the waitress to bring Leigh a beer.

"How much longer you will stay in Monterrico?" he asked.

Leigh sighed. "I don't know. I'm travelling with my friend, but it's not going well."

Alvaro raised an eyebrow. "I must be honest. I do not like this 'friend' you speak of. Each time you say 'friend,' you are not happy."

"We shouldn't be travelling together. I knew that before the trip."

"But still you came."

"Yes," she said. "It's hard to explain why. It seemed like the right decision at the time."

Renata, the cook, brought Pacífico and asked Leigh what she wanted to eat. Leigh pointed to the tacos. Alvaro ordered himself another drink and said a few things to Renata. Leigh could tell they were talking about her. Renata eventually collected Alvaro's empty bottle and walked back to the kitchen.

Alvaro looked at Leigh, apologetic. "She says you are

staying with people who live close to here. Manuel and Maria." He gestured in the direction of their property. "Renata told me she saw your friend at the beach. He was swimming, how do you say . . . dangerous?"

"I know," Leigh said. "My friend is an idiot."

"Renata, she is not happy," Alvaro said. "It is not good to swim like that here. You must know that one of the children of Maria died."

"What?"

"Just one year ago. People here, they are very careful. They are still scared. The waves . . . he broke his neck, the child. He was just twelve years old."

Leigh put down her drink. She remembered Joselito by the shore, the way he reacted when the water reached his knees. Had he seen his brother drown? Maria's face came to her mind, her clenched teeth and anguished eyes as she spoke of the waves. Justin had misunderstood. They both had.

IN THE MORNING, Leigh woke up alone in the tent. The courtyard was surprisingly quiet. They must be at church, she guessed, realizing it was Sunday. Justin's belongings were strewn about—clothes, empty cigarette packs, a notebook with nothing written inside. Without fully understanding why, she began to pack his bag. When she was done, she put it outside. Immediately, she felt better. She got dressed and walked to the outhouse. The door to the hut was slightly ajar and she could see a white comb and a spool of ribbon on the dresser. Leigh imagined

Maria standing behind her daughters in the morning, tying their braids.

She sat in the outhouse for a while, thinking. She could go to Guatemala City. Alvaro had invited her. She could also go somewhere alone, maybe find a beach where she could actually swim. Or she could keep travelling with Justin—at least he spoke Spanish.

As she pondered her options, she heard a commotion in the courtyard.

"*Te lo dije!*" A voice cried. It sounded like Maria. "*No puede nadar!*"

Leigh pulled up her shorts and went to see what was going on. Joselito was crouched in the kitchen, shielding his face. Maria held a stick in her hand. The end was charred from tending fire the night before. She raised the stick and brought it down hard on Joselito's shoulders. He screamed when the blow landed.

"Stop!" Leigh shouted. "*Por favor!*"

She positioned herself between Maria and Joselito. His hair was wet from swimming. She could see where his underwear had soaked through his pants.

"*Puta gringa!*" Maria shouted. She fastened her grip on the stick and took a swing at Leigh, muscles bulging underneath loose skin. The blow fell on Leigh's forearm. A bubble of red blood formed where she'd been hit.

"Stop!" Leigh cried.

Leigh and Maria stood facing each other with Joselito between them, hands still trying to protect his head. Maria was a mother, protecting her cub. The fear changed her face and made it softer somehow—she was beautiful. Leigh stood with her arms loose at her sides. The blood on her arm formed a meniscus and began to flow. Maria looked at Leigh, eyes narrowed. She dropped the stick and pulled her shirt down to cover her belly. "*Vete*," she said before taking Joselito inside. She locked the door behind her.

LEIGH DISMANTLED THE tent and packed her bag. She left Justin's backpack by the front gate and walked toward the beach. It was still early, but people were already setting up stands along the shore. In the distance, Leigh heard the bus trawl through town. "*Guate!*" The man yelled. "*Guate!*" With her backpack, she weaved through vendors who would spend the day selling beach clothes and mangoes carved like flowers, past men who took down boards from shack windows. Soon, someone would plug in the speakers and techno music would inundate the beach once again. Tourists would speak only of the night before, the lights and action, who slept with who.

As she neared the end of the beach, Leigh spotted Justin. He was on the lifeguard chair with a beer in his hand and a girl in his lap. She knew exactly what he would say when she arrived—*spoilsport*.

GONE TO SEED

ERIKA HASN'T HEARD FROM VIC since October when she receives his text message—*I have some-thing to ask you. Call me?* Since his son's birth, Vic has been mostly unavailable, but in the past six months he's been fully MIA. She could have called him, sure. But she's too stubborn for that, and she shouldn't have to chase after people, especially not Vic. This thing, though. It's been happening all around her—someone gets pregnant, then poof! The friend is nowhere to be seen.

She's walking up Dufferin Street, past the Mexican bakery, when she receives his message. The sweet smell of fried dough lingers in the air as she dials Vic's number, wondering what prompted him to contact her after so much radio silence.

"Baldwin!" he says, picking up on the first ring. His voice. There's a hint of laughter to it, an old familiarity that pains her. Six months apart and he answers the phone like it's been a day.

"Where have you been, Vic?" she asks.

"Oh, you know, changing diapers. Mashing turnips for Lou. That kind of thing. How are you?"

"You haven't contacted me in six months, you realize."

"That long? No way. Are you sure?"

"Yeah. Six. We had a brunch date planned right after Thanksgiving but you cancelled last minute. I haven't heard from you since. Not even during the holidays. I'm not feeling great about our friendship, Vic. Not at all."

"Sorry, sorry, I really should have called sooner. But didn't I wish you a happy New Year on Facebook?"

She remembers the message, posted publicly on her wall. A hurtful, impersonal little phrase, wishing her great success and happiness in the year to come. So generic it might've come from a fortune cookie. "That doesn't count," she tells him.

Erika hears the beep of a microwave and a muffled sound as Vic retrieves whatever's in there. "I just got busy," he says. "I don't know, I'm not good at managing my time. You know that. Everyone's mad at me. Seriously. Want a list of the angry mob? Mom's mad, Nathan's mad, Phil's super mad . . ."

Nathan, she's certain, is not mad. Neither is Phil. From what she can tell, both men had spent all kinds of time with Vic that winter. Vic's Facebook account is full of evidence—Vic and Nathan skating at Harbourfront, Vic and Phil at a sports bar in Habs jerseys, Vic and Phil and Nathan posing at a dinner party with their wives and children.

"Listen," Vic continues, "I'll explain everything tomorrow, okay? I have to go to the dentist for a root canal and they're putting me under. Apparently I can't leave without a chaperone. I need you to come with me."

"Anaesthetized? For teeth?"

"Yeah. My choice. I don't want to hear the drilling."

"Marie-Eve can't go with you?"

"No, she's in New Brunswick. Lou's with her."

"Anaesthetized? For a root canal?"

"That's what the receptionist said."

"I can't believe I haven't heard from you in so long and this is why you're calling."

"So you'll come?"

Erika hesitates, to give Vic the impression of deliberation. "I guess. But I want to see you before the dentist. You have some explaining to do."

"Want to meet at the Ship?"

"That works," she says. "Hopefully I'll still recognize you."

"Oh, I guarantee you won't. Fatherhood has rendered me hideous."

"Then I'll bring a paper bag so I don't have to look at your ugly face."

"Sounds good. Can you bring a No Frills bag? I like their logo."

"They only have plastic. You might suffocate. I'm mad, but I don't want you dead."

"No. Death would be unfortunate. Please don't be mad, Baldwin. I'm like this with everyone."

"Whatever. See you tomorrow, okay? Don't be late."

After hanging up, Erika goes into the Mexican bakery. It's a tiny storefront with room for two or three customers at a time, but she's the only person there today. Usually the churros come in orders of four, but Erika convinces the man to sell her just one. He squeezes the fresh dough directly into a vat of hot oil. It bubbles away for a few minutes as she second-guesses her decision, thinking of all the calories. But after the man fills the hot, crisp dough with *dulce de leche*, she takes a bite, no longer giving a shit about the calories.

In the streets, underneath piles of gravel, the remnants of a long and brutal winter remain trapped in the hardened snow. As she continues her walk home, an image of Vic's face appears in her mind, his Garfield-like features, something fat and cat-like about his cheeks. Those features are what made her first notice him at the laundromat on Milton Street nearly fifteen years ago, when they both lived in the McGill ghetto with all the other Jewish kids from Toronto. His face, she realizes, has been one of the only consistent presences in her adult life. And it wasn't true at all, what Vic said about being hideous. All his recent photos show him looking better than ever. His face is thinner, his hair is no longer unruly, and he wears age-appropriate clothes. Fatherhood, Erika decides, looks very good on him.

SHE ARRIVES AT the Ship twenty minutes early the next afternoon, hoping a drink will settle her nerves. She spent the morning trying to write a blog post about a particular restaurant that made her want to quit her job. Just like every other trendy restaurant on Queen West, the menu was full of over-described appetizers that would be boring if there wasn't something like a squash flower decorating the plate. Moments like that, when she realizes how much time she spends writing things that don't matter, Erika wonders if she's made any of the right decisions.

Walking into the Ship always makes her feel better. There's something comforting about the old bottles lining the walls and the cross-stitched sailors in frames that makes her feel far from her problems. Erika hasn't been there for months, mostly because it's Vic's neighbourhood and she couldn't bear the possibility of finding him there, having fun with other people. Moira, the bar's owner, waves when she realizes the grumpy-looking customer trudging through the door, accompanied by a gust of cold wind, is actually Erika.

"Love, where ya been hiding?" Moira says. "I thought you'd gone and skipped town!" Moira is one of Erika's favourite people—she's nice to everyone, has infinite patience, and refuses to lose her Irish accent even though she's been in Canada for decades.

"No, I'm still here. I've just been drinking less," Erika says. She takes off her winter jacket—hopefully she won't need it much longer—and hangs it on a hook under the counter.

"Where's Vic? You two break up or something?" Moira pours her a pint before she can explain that she's on a diet. Moira would have shushed her anyways and said, Lass, you're already skin and bones, which isn't true, but she is compared to Moira. The truth is that Erika quit drinking beer after an incident at work.

"We're just friends," Erika tells Moira. "And Vic's on his way."

The incident happened just after Christmas. "Congratulations!" Faye, a woman in advertising had exclaimed, giving Erika a hug.

"Thanks?" she'd responded, wondering if she'd received some kind of promotion someone failed to mention.

"Oh my God," Faye said. "You are glowing. Absolutely glowing. I bet your man can't keep his hands off you! That's how my husband was, just like a dog in heat. Practically sniffing my ass. They just love it, the husbands. They'll practically maul you at night when all you want to do is sleep. But you can just say, 'Honey, I'm tired,' unless you're one of those pregnant women who wants it all the time. In that case, you'll have the time of your life!"

Erika watched Faye continue to speak without picking up any social cues whatsoever and wondered how someone like her managed to keep a job.

"Actually," Erika stated at the end of Faye's soliloquy, "I'm getting an abortion."

Faye's face contorted in ways Erika never imagined possible. Instead of apologizing, she turned and half-ran down the hall. Since then, Faye refuses to even look at Erika, which suits Erika just fine.

Vic arrives at the Ship right on time, wearing properly fitting jeans and a dress shirt. His hair looks styled as well. *Six months away and look at him*, Erika thinks, though as he gets closer she can see the outline of a T-shirt underneath, probably for some obscure British punk band. Erika watches him walk through the bar, arms raised in hug position from the moment he sees her.

"Baldwin!" he says. As soon as he embraces her, she knows she won't stay mad.

"You liar," she scolds. "Shame on you. You look fabulous."

Vic shrugs. "Maybe it's the shirt."

"What's underneath? Operation Ivy?" She knows most of his band T-shirts. In fact, she'd been at many of the shows when he bought them.

He unbuttons the fancy shirt—Subhumans. She'd bought him that shirt in Montreal one summer, at Foufounes Electriques. Vic's birthday was the next day and he was too broke to buy it himself, having spent his last ten bucks on Erika's ticket because he didn't want to go alone. During the show, he gave the punk kids dirty looks when they openly judged Erika, disapproving of her thick-rimmed glasses and clothes without holes. She could always count on Vic to protect her.

"Good boy," she says. "I thought you'd turned all corporate whore."

"I've been trying to wear dad clothes. It makes Marie-Eve happy. You know that saying? Happy wife, happy life? Totally true."

"Not gonna lie, Vic. You're looking good. A bit corporate whorish, but good."

Moira pours Vic a pint and serves him a pickled egg, cuts it in half. *What a smile*, Erika thinks, watching him bite into the egg. *He's got some kind of paternal glow happening.*

"Seriously," Vic says. "What have you been up to?"

"Same old. Well, kind of. I'm going to Georgia next week."

"State or country?"

"State. I'm going to interview a tambourine player. There's this guy, Christopher Carmichael, who plays for Prince and Beck. He does gymnastics on stage and wears fur coats. I'm considering sleeping with him, if he's single. Or if he's not. Where's Marie-Eve, anyways?"

"New Brunswick. She's planting the garden. She wants us to have food when we arrive in July."

"You're still going away for two months? Even with Lou?"

"Oh yeah. We can't be in Toronto full time, no way."

"Marie-Eve flew all the way out there to plant a garden?"

"Well, she drove."

"Something wrong with the supermarket?"

"The greens are too expensive, and they're limited. We want unlimited greens."

"You guys are so weird. Who's going to take care of this garden until July?"

He shrugs. "Mother Nature."

Erika laughs. "Anyone else?"

"It'll rain. The garden will take care of itself."

"If you say so," Erika says, thinking of all the dead plants in her apartment. She's reluctant to throw them out in case they suddenly resurrect with the right watering. When she and Vic lived together, he always took care of the plants. There wasn't a wilted leaf in the house.

"She's bringing a teepee up there, too," Vic says. "I bought one off the internet."

"Why?" Erika asks, imagining a teepee tied to the roof, travelling through Quebec and along the Miramichi.

"Why not? Marie-Eve's family had a teepee growing up."

"Did she strap it to the car?"

"No, it's in a box in the trunk."

Of course Vic would buy a teepee off the internet. He had a bit of a shopping problem. In Montreal, things would arrive at least twice a week with postmarks from all over the world. He built shelves and lined them with old type-writers that didn't work and action figures that weren't really vintage even if they were advertised that way. He bought ridiculous inventions from SkyMall, like a toaster that left Darth Vader imprinted on the bread. "Jesus," she'd said to him, "I should cut up your credit cards."

Vic takes a small sip of beer. He's nursing it, trying not to drink too much because of the anaesthesia. *What the hell*, she thinks. *He's being so responsible. Marie-Eve is ruining him.*

A guy sitting at the end of the bar catches her eye and she realizes they went on a date once, probably two years ago, before she decided she'd rather die alone surrounded by cats than meet men on the internet. The guy had gone on about some start-up company involving bicycles. So many internet dates seemed to revolve around men talking about their start-up companies—she'd begun to wonder if it was a euphemism for unemployment. The best option, she decides, is to pretend she doesn't recognize him.

"I've never had anaesthesia," Vic says. "What's it like?"

"Oh God," Erika groans, remembering her first time. "It can really fuck you up. We might have to take a taxi home. Some people can't even walk afterwards. The first time I got put under, I didn't even know what I was anymore."

"You didn't *know* what you *were*?"

"Nope. I was totally out of my mind. I felt like a thing, an object. I completely lost my sense of self."

"Now you're scaring me."

"It's not so bad. Anthropologically, it's quite interest-ing. I know a girl who argued with a fire hydrant after she got her tonsils out."

Vic orders another drink. "Maybe I could fist-fight a cloud."

"Ooh," Erika says. "Living on the edge!" She orders another drink as well, but asks for a tequila and soda.

The night before, trolling photos on Facebook, Erika had been furious. How easily Vic made the decision to not call, to banish her to that place where single people go when their friends have babies. She considered texting in the middle of the night, something like *Just kidding about tomorrow. Fuck off.* She considered standing him up so he'd sit at the bar alone and remember what loneliness felt like.

Erika drinks her tequila and soda fast, not caring that she's ruining her chances of actually finishing her blog post after she leaves Vic. That restaurant, her blog, she suddenly realizes—neither actually matter. She could say anything and it would mean nothing either way.

"I'm sorry we haven't seen each other lately," Vic says.

Erika finishes her drink and orders another one. While Moira cuts a slice of lime, Erika studies her best friend. He's changed so much over the years, but she wonders if she's changed at all. When he looks at her, does he still see twentysomething Erika? The same girl who hated doing dishes and slept with too many bartenders? Possibly. Most of the time, she still feels like she's twenty-two.

"You ditched me," she says once Moira moves onto other customers. "I never in a million years thought that you, of all people, would ditch me."

"That's not—" he begins to say, stopping before *true* because he knows she's right. He tentatively reaches an arm across her shoulders. His arms, she notices, have lost the pudgy layer she used to find so comforting. She imagines him picking up Lou, the blue-eyed child she hasn't seen in so long, bouncing him toward the ceiling the way fathers do. Just last week, Lou took his first supported steps. Before long, he'd be walking. She only knew these things from the internet.

"You're my best friend," Vic says.

Erika leans against him and closes her eyes. So many times he's had his arm around her—summers at Parc Jean-Drapeau where their favourite bands played while fireworks lit up the sky, times they drank too much and needed each other to walk, and the day Erika didn't get a job she really, really wanted. Vic had taken the afternoon off work so he'd be there to celebrate when the call came— they were both certain Erika would get the position. She had freelance experience. She knew the magazine's editor. The job opening came at a time when Montreal had begun to seem unsustainable but neither she nor Vic wanted to leave. The only jobs available to them as anglophones were telemarketing, handing out promotional flyers, correct- ing film subtitles, or delivering drugs by bicycle in the McGill ghetto. "This is it," she told Vic. "It's my turn for a big break."

When the phone rang, Erika straightened her skirt, as if the person on the phone would be able to see her. "I'm sorry," the voice said. "It was a very close competition." Vic held Erika for hours while she cried—his arm must have fallen asleep. Text messages kept arriving, announc- ing themselves with a buzz, but he didn't even look. Not until Erika stopped crying. The next day, Vic woke Erika up and said it was time for them to go back to Toronto.

"I don't want to live in a place where people are too stupid to hire the smartest girl in town," he said.

"Vic," Erika says, recognizing the current of alcohol in her words. "We're drifting. I can't go another six months without you. Promise we'll never do this again."

She nuzzles closer to him and feels him tense.

"I have to tell you something," he says.

It takes Vic a moment to collect his thoughts. While she waits, Erika thinks about their second year of intense friendship. They'd become roommates by that point, inseparable. One night after dinner, he said those same words: *I have to tell you something*. She'd been standing at the ironing board, smoothing the wrinkles out of her waitressing uniform. "Sit," Vic had said, motioning to a spot beside him on the sofa. He took a deep breath and said, "I'd like to be your boyfriend." She didn't say anything as he slid a piece of paper across the table—a list of reasons why she should give him a chance. Most of them she already knew: good cook, not a broke-ass bum, knows how to fix a limited array of things but would be willing to expand that skill set. Some of them were one of a kind, like his knowledge of Morse code, which he swore might come in handy, maybe, if they were ever to be marooned together. The last reason is the one she comes back to constantly—I WOULD WRITE YOU THE BEST LOVE SONGS.

At the time, a relationship with Vic wasn't what she wanted. She loved him as a friend, but her body didn't long for him. The idea of them in bed together just seemed wrong, and the idea of potentially ruining their friendship by trying didn't seem worth the trouble. How did she even respond to him? She couldn't remember.

Over the years, he'd cooked for her anyway. Shared living costs, fixed her computer, taught her a thing or two in Morse code when they had nothing better to do. And he did write her a few love songs, mostly on summer nights when they dragged the futon mattress to the deck because it was too hot to sleep. He weaved tales of her skill in tackling moth infestations, how she only sang Elvis in the shower, how beautiful she looked in her nightgown and moccasins. Once, watching him strum a song that existed just for her, only in that moment, she almost kissed him.

"There's a reason I haven't been in touch," Vic tells her. "It has to do with Marie-Eve. She thinks there's something going on between us."

Erika tries to imagine being with Vic, their mouths against each other, lying in bed together. Now it doesn't seem so unfathomable.

"It's kind of a bad situation," Vic continues. "Just before Christmas, she found a note I wrote you and got really upset. It was an old note. One I never gave you. I guess I used it as a bookmark."

She wonders if it's the same note he'd slid across the table all those years ago—no. He said it's one he never gave her. She would give anything to know what he'd written.

"Did you tell her that?"

"I did."

"But she wasn't willing to listen. Didn't want to trust you."

"No," Vic says. "But I think enough time has passed that we can start seeing each other again. Or at least by the time we get back from New Brunswick."

Listen to this guy, she thinks. *There's an expression for this kind of behaviour—pussy-whipped.* "Oh, that's great," she says. "I'll just put my life on hold until you and Marie-Eve get your shit together." She checks her watch to avoid Vic's crestfallen face. "Looks like you're going to be late for the dentist if we don't leave now."

"I'm sorry," Vic says.

"I just wish you'd stand up for what you believe. That's what you used to do."

Vic finishes the last of his pint and they walk out of the bar together, into the cold afternoon sun. It had been Ontario's harshest winter in over a hundred years, and by January, Lake Superior had begun to freeze over. Erika checked the Weather Network every day, obsessed by the eerie satellite images of ice meeting the waves, until the entire lake froze over in February.

"What's she putting in the garden?" Erika asks Vic to fill the silence.

"All kinds of stuff. Beans, kale, carrots, beets, some lettuce. Not arugula, though. It never works. We've tried, but it's always gone to seed by the time we arrive."

In the beginning, Vic hadn't been sure about Marie-Eve. Erika was the one who convinced him to give her a chance. Even after they moved in together, Vic asked Erika to meet him at the Ship one night after Marie-Eve went to bed. He'd already been drinking. "I'm still not sure," he'd told Erika. "It's been three years. Shouldn't I know by now if she's the one?"

"Live with her a few more months," Erika had suggested. "If it's not working, leave. But you need to try."

"Do you love her?" Erika asks.

Vic stops walking and looks at her, squinting from the bright afternoon sun streaming through the web of street-car wires overhead. *We really are drifting*, she thinks. *I can't read his face at all anymore.*

"Are you serious?"

Erika looks away. "Sorry. I don't know what I'm talking about."

"Yes," he finally says. "Of course I love her."

THEY ARRIVE AT the dentist's office five minutes late. In the waiting room, a girl draws fake tattoos on her arm with a blue pen. "I want a snake," she tells her mother. "A snake and a rose."

"When you're sixteen," the mother says.

Erika hasn't been to the dentist since grad school— freelancing and short-term contracts mean no insurance. She runs her tongue over her teeth and wonders how much it would cost to get them cleaned. Vic stands beside her, asking the receptionist questions, and it occurs to Erika that she's never brought someone to the dentist before. *This is how most people live*, she realizes. *They have partners.*

"You're only getting a mould today," she hears the receptionist tell Vic.

"What do you mean?" he asks, bewildered.

"No anaesthesia. Not until the next appointment. It's a two-part process."

Vic looks at Erika and laughs. "So I can leave by myself after the appointment?"

The receptionist shoots him a quizzical look. "Of course."

Erika knows Vic expects her to leave, but she stays with him anyways. She looks over his shoulder as he scrolls through pictures on his phone and notices most of them are of his family—Lou and Marie-Eve at Cherry Beach, Marie-Eve cross-country skiing with Lou on her back. There's a candid shot of Vic passed out on the couch with Lou, mouth hanging open, head turned to the side while Lou stares into the camera, wide awake. With each photo, a growing certainty instills itself in Erika. *I want this*, she suddenly realizes. *I want that kind of life.*

Before long, the dentist calls Vic's name. He gives Erika a quick kiss on the cheek before leaving and says "Thank you." She watches him take his winter coat and head down the corridor to where the dentist will map the contours of his mouth in order to fix whatever damage needs fixing. Instead of going home, Erika remains seated in the waiting room. The teenager with the pen tattoo is called and the mother leaves, asking her daughter to text when she's done. Now Erika is alone with the receptionist who makes reminder phone calls to the next day's patients. When she's done, she smiles at Erika.

"Your husband won't be much longer," she says.

"Thank you," Erika responds, not bothering to correct the receptionist.

"He's a very kind man, your husband. Every time he comes for an appointment, he makes people laugh."

It's true, Erika thinks. Even in Montreal, he had the world laughing—friends, colleagues, random store clerks, even the ones who didn't speak much English. *People love Vic*, Erika realizes. *Everybody loves him.*

"Fifteen years ago," Erika explains to the receptionist, "he told me I should date him because he knows Morse code. Can you believe it? What a proposition."

The receptionist laughs, and before long, the two women are having a full-on conversation about their beloved husbands—where they work, how they met, which of their habits drive them crazy, and how they plan to spend their summer vacations. *This is absurd*, Erika thinks. *I shouldn't be doing this.* But as she speaks, she feels something. *This could've been my life*, she realizes. *He's loved me longer than Marie-Eve.*

"We're going to New Brunswick in July," Erika tells the receptionist, amazed at how easily she can envision their garden, thriving and wild, the arugula blowing seeds into the wind. "We go every summer."

"Do you have any children?" the receptionist asks.

"Not yet," Erika says. She hesitates and then goes for it. "But I'm expecting."

"Oh!" the receptionist cries. "I thought you might be, but it's so rude to ask! It's your first? You must be over the moon!"

Erika starts to respond but the tears come before she can finish the sentence. She sits in the empty waiting room with her hands over her face, feeling the mascara run.

"Oh," the receptionist says, changing her tone. She takes off her headset and abandons her post so she can comfort Erika, mother to mother. She puts her arms around Erika and gives her the small hug of a kind stranger. "Having a baby is overwhelming," she says. "You are going to experience so many emotions over the next few months, but you'll get through it. And you're so lucky to have a wonderful husband who will be with you every step of the way," she says, motioning to Vic who has now arrived back in the waiting room.

SHELTER FROM THE STORM

CHELSEA STOOD AT HER WINDOW, watching the city's colours change. The sky was all gunmetal clouds, a bruised aura over the horizon. Out front, a river of rain charged over a storm grate and flooded Almon Street. Everything in Halifax was at a standstill—stores had closed early, airlines cancelled flights, and everyone stayed inside, watching the drama unfold through rain-streaked windows.

The downpour reminded her of Mexico, the night she and Marco trekked through the jungle, lashing at vines, Chelsea a nervous wreck with all the glowing eyes and rustling trees. It was Marco's idea to sneak into the Palenque ruins. At dawn, before tourists flooded the site, they'd watch the sun rise through a film of early morning fog. As soon as they arrived, though, rain started to fall hard and fast. They dashed through the ruins and took shelter in the nearest temple. "Ha!" Marco laughed, wringing the water from his shirt. "*Los dioses son muy divertidos!*" The plaque over the door said TEMPLE OF THE SUN.

He would have been excited about Hurricane Juan. Chelsea imagined him swinging her around the apartment in a kind of rain dance, chanting, "*La tormenta! La tormenta!*" If only he were there instead of down south, working on a cargo ship. "Just a little longer," he told Chelsea each time the contract was extended. She couldn't exactly say no. They needed the money.

Three weeks had passed since his last call, which came from a noisy café in a Colombian port town. "*Mi estrella,*" Marco said, mouth close to the receiver. "*Eres mi media naranja*—you are the other half of my orange." She knew what he meant, but she felt like the forgotten half, dried and shrivelled on the counter. Since July, she'd been waiting. It was almost October. The week before, when she'd gone to her doctor's appointment alone, the grainy ultrasound showed everything—fingers and toes, the shape of the face. Every time Marco called she wanted to tell him the news, but there was always too much noise in the background. Eventually, she decided to wait and tell him in person. That way, there would be no mistaking his reaction.

FROM THE THIRD-FLOOR window, Patrick surveyed the graveyard of broken umbrellas on Almon Street. *Crows*, he thought. Dead crows with metal bones. Debris floated over the storm gutters—waterlogged shopping bags, mulched leaves, a wind chime from someone's porch. The whole city had shut down for Hurricane Juan, which led Orchestrata, Patrick's favourite band from LA, to cancel their show. At that exact moment, Patrick was supposed to be projecting his art, specifically designed for Orchestrata's new album using an elaborate system of colour-sound agreements, onto a space right in front of Gleb Templeton, the band's singer. Instead, he was trapped inside, held hostage by the storm like everyone else in Halifax.

Just before midnight, the city's north end lost power. Patrick lit a candle, a vigil for his lost opportunity. A marmalade glow emanated from the wick. He heard the second-floor neighbour banging open cupboards and visualized her face, often marked by a bewildered expression. Using the candle, he lit a cigarette and watched the exhale rise toward the ceiling. If his mother knew he was smoking inside, she'd be so mad. He promised he wouldn't, not ever, but certain circumstances called for bending the rules.

Out in the street, a patio chair flew into a parked car. Patrick felt a rush of excitement. That'd be on the tape. He was recording the storm for *Das Wetter*, a project he'd been working on since the spring. In the front yard, wind hammered at an oak tree. Eventually, the roots began to lift under the sidewalk. The sound it made! Splitting concrete, the tear of roots and earth! Patrick barely had time to move before the trunk crashed against the house, sending a branch straight through his window. He shielded his face as the glass exploded into his living room. The storm howled through, soaking everything in its path, including the artwork he'd created for Orchestrata.

Patrick navigated the glass minefield to gather the wet prints. He carried them to the hallway where he laid each one flat, lamenting the blurred lines and ruined colours. The phone rang, but he didn't bother answering. Soon after, he heard the back door slam on the ground floor—his mother would be up the fire escape in less than a minute. He put on his shoes and ran outside, taking two steps at a time. When their paths intercepted, his mother stared at him, face marked with worry.

"What?" he asked.

She touched the side of his face and held out her hand—blood.

LOUISE STOOD IN front of her son, shining a flashlight on his lacerated face. "Patrick!" she cried, reaching to touch the dark-red stream coming from his forehead. He dodged her hand. *The tree hit him*, she thought. *He might have a concussion. A brain injury. He might hemorrhage in the night.*

"I'm fine," Patrick muttered. "It's just a cut from the glass."

"I'm going to call an ambulance," she said.

"I'm fine," he repeated, wiping a hand across his

forehead. The blood disappeared. "Get some sleep. I'll call you in the morning."

"No—" she started to say, but Patrick was already retreating to his apartment.

She waited until she heard his door close before returning downstairs, to the home where the two of them used to live together. In the bathroom, she propped the flashlight against the sink and removed her wet clothes. In that light, she looked ghastly, with nearly translucent skin. She chose three pill bottles from the cabinet and took one from each.

In the living room, she placed a cushion on the floor and sat with her back against the wall, watching as the storm decimated her yard. Water pooled in the garden, drowning the chrysanthemums, and the wind snapped branches off the rose bush. Every sound made her nervous—debris falling on cars, toppling lawn ornaments, the pregnant neighbour's footsteps overhead. Louise held two fingers over her carotid artery, counted for ten seconds, and multiplied by six. Her pulse was much too fast.

She moved to the bedroom where she put on pyjamas and hid under the covers, waiting for the meds to make her heart feel normal again. Shadows moved across the room, and branches constantly scraped against the vinyl siding. She closed her eyes, still measuring her pulse, and prayed the storm would be over soon.

PATRICK WOKE UP the next morning feeling disoriented. His room smelled like a wet forest. *I am a wolf*, he thought. *This is my den*. He put on a shirt and looked out the broken window, past the skinned tree. The sun was full and bright and if there hadn't been so much damage, he might have mistaken the storm for a dream. He took his cigarettes from the side table and lit one. While he smoked, he felt around his face, searching for the cut.

The blood had sent his mother into a tailspin. *Jesus*, he'd wanted to say. *Chill.* He understood her concern, but the problem was that she'd been in a spell for months and he was running out of patience. She was clingy, neurotic, impossible to deal with. Despite her various illnesses, despite his best intentions, Patrick found it difficult to be nice to her. It was as though the part of his brain that made him a good son all those years had finally burned out.

On the street, people took pictures of the fallen oak. His mother was in the yard, talking to the pregnant girl from the second floor. She'd served him a few times at the Bicycle Thief. They would look each other up and down as if to say, hey, I know you, which was kind of true. They'd only ever said hello in passing, but the soundtracks of their lives sometimes collided in the vents. Eventually he'd go outside and walk around, but first he wanted to listen to his storm recording.

For months, Patrick had been learning to mimic weather conditions by drawing them. Using a wooden box with contact microphones, he was able to replicate mistral winds, flurries, drizzle, convection rainfall, and a variety of other weather conditions. The microphones would broadcast his man-made weather through the gallery while Patrick remained hidden, giving the audience a sense of how art can be simultaneously present and concealed. On November 1, he would fly to Berlin for a one-month residency in a small but reputable gallery. He had no intention of returning to Halifax afterwards.

Patrick listened to the recording and began to draw. The pencil strokes would have to be fast and angular to recreate Hurricane Juan. He thought of Basquiat—the sharp, violent lines of his paintings. Patrick laid a piece of paper on the floor and spiralled his hand fast, creating wind. Yes, there it was. Crooked rain, high winds. Patrick could feel his body responding to the soundtrack—his breath came in raw gusts and he felt the synchronicity of everything.

This is it, Patrick thought. *I was born to do this.*

CHELSEA AWOKE WITH the shape of Marco's name in her mouth. She'd been dreaming of Isla Holbox again. For three days it had rained. On the fourth, the sun returned, casting its reflection on the knee-deep puddles left behind. Chelsea and Marco had borrowed bicycles from the hotel and ridden to the far side of the island, pedalling hard through mud. They left their clothes on the shore and made love in a shallow bay, sand clouding around Chelsea's knees as she straddled Marco. In the distance, two flamingos stood near the shore with their backs turned, elegantly facing the sun. She'd been home a month when she realized she hadn't menstruated for some time. The doctor confirmed the date—the child had been conceived that afternoon.

How quickly weather can turn, Chelsea thought. She stood at the window and watched birds side-wind through the sky, a second ocean. It smelled like spring again. In the yard below, ravaged branches from the fallen tree covered the grass. The old yellow of last week's fall mingled with new and vibrant greens. The landlord was there, raking leaves into a pile. When she noticed Chelsea, she motioned for her to come down. Chelsea put on a sweater that would hide her stomach before descending the stairs.

"Everything okay up there?" the landlord asked.

"The apartment's fine," Chelsea confirmed. "Thanks."

Disappointment flickered across the landlord's face as she motioned toward the fallen oak. "My husband planted that tree when Patrick was young. When he got older, he'd climb up there and draw all day. I could never get him to come down for dinner."

"I'm sorry," Chelsea said.

Louise stopped raking for a moment. She gave Chelsea a once-over, blue eyes squinting as if looking for some hidden truth. Her eyes travelled down to Chelsea's bulky sweater.

"Your boyfriend," she said. "Where'd you say he is? Chile?"

"Colombia."

"Wasn't he supposed to be here this summer?"

"Something came up," Chelsea said. "He's coming soon."

After their conversation, Chelsea returned to her apartment and lay on her bed, curtains drawn. It wasn't the first time the landlord had mentioned something about Marco in a way that suggested he didn't exist or wasn't coming. Since returning to Halifax, Chelsea hadn't really connected with anyone. None of her old friends, no one at work seemed to understand. She barely even talked to her parents anymore. Whenever anyone found out she'd only known Marco for a few months, their faces betrayed the words they wouldn't dare speak: *That child will have no father.*

LOUISE TOOK A nap after lunch. The covers over her body felt like the lead vest patients wear during X-rays. It reminded her of a game Patrick once played with her called sandman. "Concentrate," he'd said. "You are in your bed. It's deep summer and the windows are open. While you're sleeping, the sandman comes through the window. He is standing over you. He has a knife in his hand and begins to cut you. He is cutting from heel to toe. Now he is folding back skin. He is filling your foot with warm, heavy sand . . ." Patrick went through each part of Louise's body. He took out her eyes and filled the cavities with sand. He cut a hole in her head the way one would a jack-o'-lantern. When he told Louise to open her eyes, she was pinned to the ground.

His power over her was frightening. Louise felt his headaches in her temples, his rage in her stomach. It had been like that even before she lost her husband, but it intensified when she was left to raise Patrick alone. Once, she tried to explain how she was tuned into his frequency. His reaction was that of a despot humouring a fool.

Their relationship was changing. First, Patrick had announced he wanted to move to Europe. "All good art happens in Berlin," he'd claimed with the pompous certainty of a late teenager. Louise had tried deterring him by using conventional methods of guilt: "What about your education? What about money? More importantly, what will I do without you?"

She didn't want to be irrational or manipulative, but both seemed necessary given the circumstances. Louise picked vasovagal syncope because the symptoms were elusive and the disease was easy to simulate. A fainting episode while jogging, another in the kitchen, one triggered by gunshots on TV and she had herself a bona fide medical disorder. Patrick immediately inundated her with questions: "What is your doctor doing to narrow the pathology? Did you ask about the nerve conduction test? Can't you get a scan?" As months passed and Louise remained uncured, Patrick began to lose interest. In May, when the third-floor tenant moved out, Patrick asked to move in. "I need space," he said. If she didn't agree, he'd go elsewhere. Imagine. Blackmailed by her own son.

With every utterance, Louise felt their mother-son helix unravel. Pieces were missing in his goodbye hugs. He must have known she would detect it, agonize over it. For what reason? Maybe he already knew she'd been lying to him. Maybe that was his revenge.

IN THE EARLY afternoon, Patrick heard a knock at the back door. "Hello?" a voice said—not his mother. He crossed the apartment and was surprised to see the girl from the second floor. She wore a baggy sweater with a wolf on it, something he might wear.

"I'm out of sugar," she said, offering coffee in exchange.

He directed her to a small jar of sugar on the counter. She stirred a spoonful into her cup and followed him down the hall, stepping over his Orchestrata prints, wrinkled from water damage. Before sitting down in his only chair, she scanned his record collection, alphabetized in crates along the wall, and perused the graveyard of electronic equipment to be used for various projects or perhaps nothing at all. Patrick crouched with his elbows on his knees, frayed white holes framing his kneecaps.

"What kind of person are you?" she asked him. "I mean, if you had to define yourself."

Patrick was surprised by her forwardness. After a moment, he said, "I would say I'm ruminative. Often perplexed. Most of the time, I feel like the sound a mouth harp makes."

She laughed.

"How does it feel?" he asked, pointing to her belly.

"Strange," Chelsea said, pulling at her sweater to hide the bump. "Nerve-racking."

"Nerve-racking?"

"My boyfriend doesn't know yet."

Patrick raised his eyebrows. "No?"

"He's away. I want to tell him in person."

"Right."

"He'll be here soon," she added.

"Are you scared?" Patrick asked.

"No," she responded. She reconsidered. "Yes."

Patrick swirled his coffee and peered into the bottom. "The grains in this cup tell me your future will be golden."

"I hope you're right," Chelsea said.

LATER THAT AFTERNOON, they explored the storm-ravaged city together. "Quick, before my mother sees," Patrick said, ushering Chelsea down the fire escape. They followed Agricola Street to the Commons, past torn vinyl siding and shingles from a blown-off roof. Military trucks lined the road by the public gardens and uniformed men stood in front of a roped-off area.

"You'd think this was the zombie apocalypse or something," Patrick said.

Debris was piled as high as snowbanks on Barrington Street. At the waterfront, a barefoot man told a crowd that during the hurricane, he'd seen the face of God in the waves. Bright-pink tape blocked sections of the boardwalk but people stepped over to take photos of a sunken ship. The tip of the mast rose just above the water's surface. Below, you could make out the ship's deck with its furled ropes and waterlogged crates.

"My boyfriend's a sailor," Chelsea told Patrick.

She'd first met Marco in Veracruz, early one morning at the fish market. From a barnacle-crusted dock, she watched the returning boats trawl across the flat morning surface. Marco was at the hull of one of those ships. He looked at Chelsea across the water and if she hadn't believed in love at first sight before, that moment changed her mind.

A friend of Patrick's sauntered down the wharf, waving to get his attention. Chelsea recognized the boy from the Bicycle Thief, where she had too often served him and his drunk friends. Sometimes, late at night, he flirted. He didn't recognize her out of context.

"Heard about Orchestrata," he said, slapping Patrick on the back. "Bummer! When are they back?"

"Doesn't matter. I'll be in Germany."

"Right. You been to Point Pleasant yet? I hear it's fucked. I have my mom's car if you want a ride."

When she was a child, before the family moved up-island, Chelsea's parents had often taken her to Point Pleasant on Sundays. Later, when she moved back for university, she and her friends drank there on Friday nights. Sometimes they wrote messages on torn bits of cigarette packs and sent their hopeful bottles floating into the harbour.

Patrick and Chelsea walked to where his friend had parked and they drove away from the city centre, detouring once where a fallen tree had tangled with the power lines. Traffic gridlocked as soon as they turned onto Point Pleasant Drive. They pulled over and entered the far end of the park.

It was hard to follow any one trail because of the damage so they zigzagged through the remains of what had once been a lush forest. A scent hung in the air, a mixture of splintered wood, gasoline, and the sea. Almost every tree had been pushed over, broken, or uprooted. Jagged trunks scraped the horizon and the ocean's deep blue framed the newly empty spaces.

"This is fucked," Patrick agreed, taking pictures.

Chelsea gazed at the ocean, now calm, and thought of her Sunday walks through those trees. Her parents would be devastated. They'd called her in the morning but she let it go to the answering machine. On the message, her mom asked if she was okay and recounted disaster stories from the paper. She also said they'd be driving down from Sydney on the weekend. Chelsea hadn't seen them in two months. Not since she started showing.

"No excuses this time," her mother said. "We're coming and that's final."

LOUISE WATCHED HER son sneak off with the girl from the second floor and it occurred to her that Patrick might be the father. There was something disconcerting about their body language as they trotted down the fire escape. Something secretive. Also, the girl looked five or six months pregnant. That was about how long Patrick had been distancing himself. Ever since the girl moved in, she kept saying her "boyfriend" was coming. "He's in Panama," she said once. The next time he'd be in Brazil or somewhere equally implausible. His arrival was either delayed because of paperwork or some job he had to do. The story changed every time.

Louise decided the only option was to find evidence and confront him. Patrick's door was locked but she had her own key. She hadn't been inside for weeks and was annoyed to find the apartment in deplorable condition—dirty dishes sagged in piles on the kitchen counter. Some of them were grey-streaked and smelled like cigarettes. The living room was in disarray, and not just because of the tree and the broken window. Her first thought: *I'll evict him.*

As she stood in the centre of the room, Louise began to feel strange. She steadied herself against an armchair. It wasn't so much the state of the apartment as the realization that Patrick had grown up to be just like his father. The mess, the records in milk crates, the smoking, his artistic tendencies. Even their beards were similar. Her vision started to blur. She straightened the sheets on Patrick's bed and decided to lie down for a moment. His scent had changed now that he was doing his own laundry, buying his own soap.

Beside Patrick's bed was his Moleskine notebook. When she picked it up, a few papers slid out—a ticket to Germany for November 1st and some documents. There were English subtitles in small italic font below the German. Name, address, date of birth. Date of arrival. Next of kin. The forms, she realized, were for some kind of visa.

Tears sprang into Louise's eyes. His departure was only a month away and he hadn't mentioned the trip, not one thing about it. What was wrong with him? Whatever the story was, she decided, Patrick wasn't going anywhere. Louise took his plane ticket and the papers and tore them in half. She ripped again and again, tearing until there was nothing left but a pile of scraps.

BEFORE LONG, DARKNESS was upon the city again. Chelsea and Patrick walked along Almon Street, talking to people who drank warm beer in the twilight and exchanged disaster stories. Someone had set up a generator on the sidewalk. A small group crowded around a television, watching that evening's episode of *Survivor*. In the yard next door, neighbours pooled their perishables and cooked them over a communal fire. The air smelled of burnt marshmallows and steak.

"Hey," one of the neighbours asked, "are you hungry?"

"I'm okay," Chelsea replied. She was starving, but her ankles hurt. All she wanted to do was lie down. Patrick declined the offer as well. He opened the back gate and let Chelsea go first. Thick, leafy branches lay in haphazard patterns on the waterlogged grass and Louise's sneakers, still wet from the night before, dangled from a makeshift clothesline.

"When do you leave for Germany?" Chelsea asked.

"November first."

"When are you back?"

"I'm not."

"Never?"

"Not if I can help it. Don't say anything if my mom asks."

"She doesn't know?"

"I can't tell her. She's crazy."

"Like, mother crazy, or crazy-crazy?"

"Both."

"You're seriously going to take off without saying anything?"

"That's the plan."

"Have you considered what it'll do to her?"

"It's better this way, trust me."

Chelsea crossed her arms. "I hope I don't have a kid like you," she said.

Patrick continued up the fire escape while Chelsea fumbled for her keys. She entered her dark apartment and lit two candles. She walked down the hallway to the bedroom, trying not to let the wax drip. By the time she changed into her pyjamas, there was a lot of noise overhead. She heard both Patrick's and Louise's voices. Various snippets of disjointed arguments and accusations percolated through the vent. Chelsea fought the urge to go upstairs—it wasn't her place to intervene. Still, she felt sorry for the landlord and the overblown, uncontrollable love she had for her son. It marred her judgement and left her vulnerable.

Chelsea got into bed with her notebook. *Today, I saw a sunken boat at the harbour and thought of you*, she wrote. *I remember your stories of mayday calls, water in your lungs, and I never want you to be that way. I want you the way we were in Isla Holbox, together, legs entwined beneath the water. I told my neighbour that you're a sailor. Know what he said? Sometimes sailors don't come back to port. Prove him wrong, Marco. Please.*

She put the notebook aside. Lying on her back, she felt the extra weight in every part of her body. Even her hands felt fat. Soon, the baby would be kicking, doing somersaults. On Friday, her parents would arrive in Halifax. Her mother would know immediately.

She was almost asleep when she heard a new kind of noise upstairs—a sharp cry. When she heard it again, she got dressed and went up the fire escape. Through the window she saw Louise, tied to a chair with a gag in her mouth. Patrick was pacing in front of her, smoking a cigarette.

Chelsea opened the door.

"Patrick—"

"She doesn't like it when the paramedics come," he interrupted. He crouched in front of his mother and smoothed back her hair. Louise screamed through the rag while Patrick shushed her. Underneath the restraints, her feet kicked. Chelsea looked at his arms. He was thin to have tied up a grown woman. She wondered how many times he'd done it in the past.

The doorbell rang. Chelsea looked at Patrick and realized he was crying. She walked to the livingroom window and saw the revolution of red and blue lights in the street. A few people stood nearby, waiting to see what would happen. Chelsea went downstairs to unlock the door for the paramedics while Patrick stayed with Louise. She started to follow them back upstairs but changed her mind. From her own window, she watched Louise come out on the stretcher with Patrick following close behind. Before he got into the ambulance, he looked up and caught Chelsea's eye. It was difficult to guess what his expression was meant to tell her, but she immediately regretted what she'd said—*I hope I don't have a kid like you.*

PATRICK STAYED AT the hospital until the doctor insisted he get some rest. He took a taxi home and stood on the lawn for a while, looking at the fallen oak, a tree planted by a father he didn't remember. He'd drawn his first picture up in those branches. He climbed the stairs and lay on his bed, surrounded by what had once been his plane ticket and visa. In his Moleskine, he scrawled a reminder to print new copies once the library reopened. The night air through the broken window was fresh and crisp and he stayed up the rest of the night, drawing wind and rain by candlelight, thinking about Germany. He wondered whether or not he'd ever get there. Downstairs, Chelsea fell asleep to someone playing "Shelter from the Storm" at the bonfire next door. In her dreams, she was a mother, holding her baby close in a soft blue blanket.

THAT SAME NIGHT, thousands of kilometres away, a cargo ship docked in Puerto Escondido. A gang of unshaven sailors, filthy from weeks at sea, filed down the ship's worn ramp and staggered a little when their feet hit land. They walked through the shipyard and headed for the nearest cantina to finish the night with women and mezcal. One of the men, however, did not follow. He said a quiet goodbye to his crew and walked north to hail a taxi.

"*Adónde vas?*" the driver asked, yawning.

"*Al aeropuerto,*" Marco told the driver.

He put his bag in the trunk and slid into the back seat. The taxi drove fast through green lights while the red digits from the meter reflected on the dashboard. Marco reached into his pocket and took out a paper with the address 122 ALMON STREET, HALIFAX, NOVA SCOTIA written on it. His new home. There was something else in his pocket—a ring. A small silver one he'd been carrying for months. On the inside, engraved in small, cursive writing, was a phrase, a promise—MI MEDIA NARANJA.

ACKNOWLEDGEMENTS

First and foremost, I'd like to thank the *New Quarterly* for their continued support. Extra special thanks to Susan Scott, Kim Jernigan, and Pamela Mulloy for being particularly incredible. Two stories from this manuscript, "Waiting for the Cyclone" and "Shelter from the Storm," first appeared in their pages.

Thanks to SSHRC, the Toronto Arts Council, the Ontario Arts Council, and Canada Council for financially supporting me while I wrote and researched this book.

Thanks to Taryn Boyd, Colin Thomas, Pete Kohut, and everyone at Brindle & Glass for being awesome, and making my book cover beautiful.

A big thank you to Samantha Haywood, my agent, for her confidence and insightful advice.

Thanks to my wise mentors: Catherine Bush, Caroline Adderson, Michael Winter, Josip Novakovitch, Russell Smith, and Sina Queryas.

Gratitude for my readers/editors: Alexia Papadopoulis, Lauren Stein, Julia Campbell-Such, Roseanne Harvey, Jon Harding, Emily Wilson, Jack Allen, Michael Juretic, Nick McArthur, and everyone who critiqued my work during the University of Guelph MFA program.

Thanks to past housemates Efrat Gold, Cosima Herter, and Rachel Cameron for their friendship and for putting up with my less than desirable behaviour while I wrestled with this manuscript. A special thanks to Meghan McKiernan and Ashley Weese for giving me wine and scheduling sleepovers when I needed a break.

Thanks to my ninety-four-year-old grandmother, Margaret Sanche, who still reads everything I publish and brags about me in her housing complex.

Thanks to Ayelet Tsabari for modelling how to write about badass women and for making me look good in my headshots.

Thanks to Selkirk College, especially Almeda Glenn Miller, Renee Jackson-Harper, and all my creative writing students. We are creating something wonderful here in the Kootenays.

Much love to Will Johnson, aka Literary Goon, and my irreplaceable platonic life partner Kathy Friedman, for their wisdom, companionship, and editorial suggestions.

Love and gratitude to my mother, Theresa Dean, who unfortunately passed away before I could finish this book.